THE DREAM AND THE GLORY

Barbara Cartland, the celebrated romantic novelist, historian, playwright, lecturer, political speaker and television personality, has now written over two hundred books. She has had a number of historical books published and several biographical ones, including a biography of her brother, Major Ronald Cartland, who was the first Member of Parliament to be killed in the war. The book has a preface by Sir Winston Churchill.

In private life, Barbara Cartland is a Dame of Grace of St John of Jerusalem, and one of the first women, after a thousand years, to be admitted to the Chapter General. Chairman of the St John Council in Hertfordshire, she has served in the St John Ambulance Brigade for thirty-five years.

Barbara Cartland has fought for better conditions and salaries for midwives and nurses, and, as President of the Hertfordshire Branch of the Royal College of Midwives, she has been invested with the first Badge of Office ever given in Great Britain, which was subscribed to by the midwives themselves. She has also championed the cause of old people and founded the first Romany Gypsy Camp in the world. It was christened 'Barbaraville' by the gypsies.

Barbara Cartland is deeply interested in Vitamin Therapy and is President of the National Association for Health.

D1138254

By the same author in Pan Books

For other titles by Barbara Cartland
please see page 155

BARBARA CARTLAND

THE DREAM
AND THE GLORY

Pan Original

Pan Books London and Sydney

First published 1977 by Pan Books Ltd,
Cavaye Place, London SW10 9PG
© 1977 Cartland Promotions and The Order of St. John
ISBN 0 330 24853 7
Printed and bound in Great Britain by
Hazell Watson & Viney Ltd, Aylesbury, Bucks

Author's Note

On September 19th 1798 the British Fleet, after their triumphant victory at the Battle of the Nile, blockaded the French in Malta. The Siege continued for exactly a year.

Napoleon Bonaparte had forced the Knights to leave Malta, but the Order was not destroyed and its valiant spirit remained as invincible and dedicated as it had been since the Crusades.

It was revived in England in 1831, and in 1877 the St. John Ambulance Brigade was finally established.

The Ophthalmic Hospital in Jerusalem was opened in 1882.

Today Priories of the British Order are active in Scotland, Wales, South Africa, Canada, New Zealand and Australia. There are Commanderies in Western Australia, Northern Ireland and Central Africa. There is also an American society of the Order.

The great ideal and the spirit of selfless dedication started by a few monks at the Pilgrim Hostel in Jerusalem in A.D. 800 has carried on down the ages until today there are 263,267 members of the St. John Ambulance Brigade working in 31 countries of the world.

Few people realise that Master Mariners and policemen must qualify for a First Aid Certificate and that the Ambulance and Nursing Members in their black and white uniforms who man the First Aid Posts in factories and theatres and who are present at all sports rallies, football matches, protest marches, riots and public demonstrations are unpaid.

For the Service of Mankind these men and women give their most valuable possession – themselves and their time.

This is the vision and the dream for which the Knights of the Order have lived and died for a thousand years and through their inspiration and example there will always be young idealists to follow the eight-pointed cross.

I am very grateful for the help and collaboration of Miss Pamela Willis, Curator of the Order, St. John's Gate, Clerkenwell, London, EC1.

Dedication

I dedicate this novel to the most amazing phenomenon in this materialistic age – the Members of the St. John Ambulance Brigade, who, from the voluntary unpaid Commander-in-Chief to the youngest cadet, ceaselessly and magnificently live up to their motto "For the Service of Mankind".

Chapter One
1798

"How much longer will we have to stay here?"

There was a note of impatience in the man's voice as he stood looking over the Bay of Naples.

It was impossible to imagine that anything could be more lovely than the view from the Palazzo Sessa where the British Ambassador lived.

The flat façades of peach and cream-coloured plaster rising from the terraces, the stately walls of the Royal Palace to the left, the Castle dell'Ovo supposed to have been built on a magic egg supplied by the wizard Vergil, all looked as if they were part of a fairy-tale.

And ahead was the misty blue island of Capri and the exquisite coastline fading away into the distance beneath the smouldering cone of Mount Vesuvius.

"They expect a ship any day," a soft voice replied and Lady Cordelia Stanton moved across the marble-paved terrace to stand beside her brother looking out onto the Bay.

She knew that she could never be discontented with the azure sky reflected in the blue-green sea, with the light gilding the crowded shipping in the harbour and black cypress trees standing like sentinels on the slopes above the town.

She had never dreamt, Cordelia thought, that there could be such a profusion of colour as she had found in the gardens of Naples.

The purity of the orange blossoms, the mass of roses, syringa and oleander vied with the star-shaped white flowers of the myrtle, the scented rosemary and the purple bougainvillaea.

She had expected Naples to be beautiful, but not to contain all the elements of magic which she had thought existed only in her imagination.

"We have been here for nearly three weeks," her brother said in an irritated tone.

"It is unlike you to complain, David," Cordelia said gently, "and Sir William and Lady Hamilton have been so kind."

"I appreciate that but you know, Cordelia how much I long to reach Malta. To me every inch of the journey here has been a crusade, and now my Holy Land is within reach."

The throb of emotion in his voice made Cordelia put out her hand and lay it on his arm.

"I know what you are feeling, dearest," she said, "but I cannot help remembering that when you are a Knight of St. John you will leave me behind."

There was a moment's silence, before the young Earl of Hunstanton asked in a very different tone:

"Am I being incredibly selfish in not looking after you?"

"No, of course not!" Cordelia said hastily. "We have discussed that many times and we agreed that we both have our own lives to lead. That you should be a Knight has been your ambition ever since you were a tiny child."

"That is true," the Earl replied. "I can remember Mama telling me stories about the Crusades. How valiantly the Crusaders fought against the Saracens, then in all humility the Knights Hospitallers nursed the wounded of both armies in their hospital in Jerusalem!"

There was a pause before he said:

"That is true Christianity, Cordelia, and that is the ideal to which I have dedicated myself ever since I can remember."

"Yes, I know," Cordelia replied, "but if I return to England, Malta will seem very far away."

"If?"

Her brother turned to look at her.

"You said – if. Are you considering what I suggested?"

"Yes, David, but I do not wish to speak of it now. We were talking about you and you are waiting for a ship."

He smiled at her and it seemed to illuminate his young face.

"I have been waiting for what has seemed to me to be centuries," he replied, "although actually it is only three years: first to hear if my application to the Grand Master had been accepted – then for Papal approval, and now just for ordinary transportation to carry me to where I can make my vows."

He turned away from his sister as he finished speaking to look once again over the shimmering sea, as if he expected to see a ship coming into Port bearing on its sails the great eight-pointed cross of the Knights of the Order of St. John.

However, although there were many ships moving in and out of one of the busiest Ports in the Mediterranean, there was not the one he sought.

Cordelia gave a sigh and walked a little way from her brother to touch with gentle fingers the pink camellias which were peeping through the stone balustrade.

She resembled a flower herself in her white muslin gown with its soft frilled fichu, her small waist encircled with a blue sash.

Despite the warmth of the sunshine she was not wearing a hat, and the sunlight glinted on the pale gold hair which framed in fashionable curls her small pointed face.

Her eyes were very large and dark-fringed, and unexpectedly, when they should have been blue, they were grey with a touch of purple.

They were unusual eyes which gave her face a piquancy and a mystery that is often lacking in a very young girl's expression.

Ever since she had come to Naples Cordelia had been complimented and feted by the black-eyed Patricians who lived in elaborate Palaces carved with ornate coats-of-arms.

They could only be glimpsed through high gilt traceried gates which separated the flower-filled Court-yards from the curious populace.

Fountains splashed in the marble basins and carved Tritons blew conches beneath the cool, elegant Salons whose occupants discussed nothing but conspiracies, treachery and the French warships in Toulon.

Cordelia thought sometimes that it had been a mistake to come to Naples when all Europe was in a fever of anxiety and England was now alone, with no allies, opposing Bonaparte.

He was like a monster darkening every land with his shadow.

But once her brother knew that his application to become a Knight of St. John had been accepted, nothing short of death would have kept him away from his 'Promised Land'.

It seemed strange that as Earl of Hunstanton, with a great Estate in Berkshire, with a family home in London, and several other properties scattered over the British Isles, he should wish to renounce everything to become a Knight.

But, as he had said himself, it had been his goal and ambition ever since a child.

Now with both their parents dead, he was his own master and nothing could have prevented the Earl reaching Malta.

It had been an opportunity for Cordelia to see the fashionable world from which she had been excluded through mourning until the beginning of the year.

She found herself enjoying the Balls, the theatres, assemblies and Receptions which she had attended since reaching Naples.

She had been afraid of meeting Lady Hamilton, the British Ambassadress of whom she had heard so many fantastic stories and whose beauty was a legend.

But Emma Hamilton had shown her only kindness, and her irresistible vitality had swept aside Cordelia's shyness from the moment she arrived at the Palazzo Sessa.

Nearing forty, Lady Hamilton, whose life-story had caused a great deal of whispering amongst the aristocratic Neapolitans, was still overwhelmingly lovely.

Whilst at Cordelia's age she had been slim, graceful and with an angelic beauty which only the artist George Romney could depict in its perfection, now her figure had lost its fawn-like slimness.

But she was still amazingly beautiful and her Grecian attitudes, which had been one of the attractions of the Capital, were just as compelling.

"She is fascinating ... absolutely fascinating!" Cordelia had said to her brother a dozen times.

But she had known that David would not allow his mind to linger on the beauty of any woman when he was about to take the vow of chastity together with those of poverty and obedience.

Cordelia was entranced by everything she found in this fantastic world of fashion.

There was the Queen with her smooth pink-and-white Hapsburg complexion, who made up for what she lacked in looks by her stupendous jewels, elaborate gowns, feathers and furs, combined with a Royal air which over-awed most people, especially her ineffective, rather stupid husband.

His Majesty King Ferdinand IV paid Cordelia extravagant compliments, which amused rather than embarrassed her.

She realised that he cared nothing for what happened to anyone else as long as he was left undisturbed to enjoy his appetite for food and to indulge in any pleasure which caught his fancy.

He was quite unlike any King that Cordelia had ever imagined.

He liked to catch fish in the Bay and sell them in the market-place in Naples, haggling shrewdly over the price with the local fishermen.

He especially enjoyed macaroni, which he ate with his fingers. Cordelia had seen him throw a handful of it from his box at the Opera onto the crowd below.

But he was afraid of his Queen and in order to escape from her passionate hysterics and her scathing tongue he had handed over to her every Department of State, and was not in the least ashamed of it.

The person whom Cordelia liked best in Naples was Sir William Hamilton.

Growing old, he found that the tension of politics and the rumours which swept Naples into a sense of frenzy every other day bored him.

Instead he spent his time enjoying the treasures of antiquity which he had accumulated in the Embassy and was utterly absorbed in his Grecian urns and the new discoveries at Pompeii, which were ignored by the majority of the upper-class Neapolitans.

Sir Willian had been only too pleased to have a new pupil in the shape of Cordelia.

It seemed years now since he had instructed the lovely Emma when she had been sent to him as his mistress and whom, because she was the most perfect treasure in all his collection, he had made his wife.

Cordelia exclaimed with delight over his collection of old bronzes and his cabinets of ivories and coins.

"Tell me about the Greeks when they came to Naples," Cordelia would ask.

She would bring the light of youth back into the Ambassador's eyes, and a note of excitement into his tired old voice as he told her everything she wanted to hear.

Immersed though he was in the past, even Sir William could not ignore the rising tension within Naples, and his anxiety had communicated itself to Cordelia so that now she glanced at her brother nervously, wondering if she dare tell him of her fears.

"David ..." she began with an urgent note in her voice. Then at that moment they were interrupted.

A man came through the open windows of the Salon onto the terrace and stood for a moment looking first at Cordelia, then at her brother.

David was still staring out to sea and was unaware that anyone had joined them, but Cordelia moved forward politely.

She realised that as Lady Hamilton was at the Palace with the Queen, she must play the part of hostess.

She noticed that the new arrival was tall and square-shouldered.

He was fashionably, if somewhat carelessly dressed, and she was sure, as she approached him, that he was English.

There was no mistaking his air of superiority – or was it one of command?

He had fair hair above a face burnt so brown by the sun that she might in fact have questioned his English blood, had it not been that in contrast his eyes were vividly, dazzlingly blue.

He had, she thought, looked a little stern when he first appeared, but as she curtsied he smiled and it made him look extremely attractive.

Yet at the same time she was aware that he had a raffish, almost mocking expression which for the moment she could not quite place.

Then as he took her hand in his she knew what it was.

He looked like a buccaneer, a man such as Drake and Hawkins who had dominated the seas in their ships and whose modern counterparts still were harrying the Barbary Pirates.

"Good afternoon," Cordelia said. "I am afraid Lady Hamilton is not at home, but she will be returning shortly."

"I think it is really you I have come to see," the stranger replied.

She had been right. He was English and he had a deep voice which was arresting and was in fact a relief to listen to after the high quick chatter of the Neapolitans.

Cordelia looked at him in surprise and he continued:

"Can you possibly be the freckle-nosed little cousin I remember storming at me in a passionate rage because accidentally I had shot one of her doves?"

"Mark!" Cordelia exclaimed. "Cousin Mark!"

"I see you have remembered!"

He put out his hand and she laid her fingers in his.

Mark Stanton, she thought incredulously, was the last person she would have expected to see at this moment, for they had not met for at least nine years.

The Earl of Hunstanton turned from his contemplation of the sea.

Then he gave a shout of delight.

"Mark!" he cried. "How splendid that you are here. I had no idea you were in the Mediterranean."

"I was far more surprised to hear that you require my services," his cousin answered. "I have often thought of you in England, safe and secure at Stanton Park, but now I learn you wish to visit Malta."

"Not visit," the Earl said quickly. "I am to be a Knight, Mark. They have accepted me!"

For a moment the blue eyes looked astonished, then Mark Stanton put his hand on his cousin's shoulder.

"I remember your saying when you were a boy that that

was what you wished to be. But I thought perhaps it was one of those things you would forget as you grew older."

He paused to add with a twinkle in his eye:

"Or find yourself side-tracked by more alluring amusements."

"This is not in the nature of an amusement, Mark," the Earl said a little stiffly. "I wish to dedicate myself to the service of Christ, and how could I do it better than by being a Knight of St. John?"

Cordelia, watching their cousin, thought that he was about to reply somewhat frivolously, but instead he said with what she thought was a beguiling smile:

"Suppose we sit down and you tell me about it?"

His words made her remember her manners.

"Will you come into the Salon?" she asked. "It is very hot out here and I am sure the servants have refreshments ready for you."

There was in fact wine which was poured into large crystal glasses engraved with the British coat-of-arms, and there were small cakes, sandwiches and other delicacies which were always provided at the Palazzo Sessa.

They seated themselves on comfortable satin sofas which embellished the huge Salon where Lady Hamilton performed.

There was a piano on which she was accompanied while she sang duets with the King, and there were several of Sir William's priceless Etruscan vases against which she stood or knelt to become in that moment as classical and memorable as the vases themselves.

Mark Stanton was looking at Cordelia, and the expression in his blue eyes made her feel shy.

"Tell me why you are here ..." he began, only to be interrupted by the Earl.

"Am I to understand from what you said when you arrived," he asked, "that you can take us to Malta?"

"I have brought my ship into Port for a small repair," Mark Stanton replied.

"*Your* ship?"

"I speak as the Captain of it. It is actually the property of a Knight."

"A ship of the Order!" the Earl exclaimed excitedly. "Do you hear, Cordelia? Mark has a ship here at this moment in which he can carry us to Malta!"

Cordelia looked at her cousin and he said:

"I am afraid you will have to wait a day or so. The Turks have made a hole in the hull which must be repaired before we can go any further."

"You have been in an engagement?" the Earl asked. "What happened?"

Captain Mark Stanton smiled.

"What do you think? We took a number of prisoners and a valuable cargo."

David Hunstanton gave a sigh of sheer happiness.

"Another blow against the Infidel!" he said. "How I wish I had been with you!"

"It was not a very glorious victory," Captain Stanton said with the mocking note in his voice. "The Turkish ship was smaller than ours, but he did try to disguise his nationality."

"Why should he do that?"

"The Great Powers have made a number of treaties and contracts with our traditional enemies," Mark Stanton explained. "At one time every boat licensed in Malta was allowed to attack Moslem shipping."

"And quite right!" the Earl interposed.

"The Order," Captain Stanton continued, "provided the basic facilities on the Island for vessels of many nationalities apart from their own. In return all the booty was sold in Malta and the Order took ten per cent of the proceeds."

"It sounds very commercial," the Earl said doubtfully.

"The Knights of St. John are heroes, not saints!" his cousin replied, and now there was no mistaking the laughter in his voice.

Cordelia glanced at him quickly.

She hoped he would not tease David or indeed argue with him about his determination to be a Knight.

They had gone over the whole idea so often, they had

endured a great deal of opposition from their relatives; but nothing and nobody, she knew, would divert her brother from his intended course.

'I could not bear to have it discussed all over again,' she thought to herself. 'Besides, it upsets David.'

"Now things are very different," Mark Stanton was saying. "French ships trading in the Levant are immune from attack by the Knights of St. John even if they are carrying Turkish goods. The Turks make every effort to acquire French Passports."

"But you still sail along the African coast?" the Earl asked quickly.

"We do that," his cousin agreed, "and we never cease in our efforts to rescue Christian slaves."

"Are there still thousands in Algiers and Tangier?" Cordelia asked.

"I am afraid so," Mark Stanton replied. "But you will find an enormous number of slaves in Malta also."

Cordelia looked startled and he said :

"Malta was at one time one of the biggest slave markets in Europe. Two hundred slaves or more are still captured almost every year. The Sultan buys back a large number of them at 100 louis a time!"

"I am not interested in slaves," the Earl interrupted, "although I understand they are part of the booty. Tell me about your ship. How can you be the Captain of one which belongs to the Order if you are not yourself a Knight?"

"The ship I am commanding at the moment," Mark Stanton replied, "is the private property of Baron Ludwig von Wütenstein of the Anglo-Bavarian Langue, which I imagine you yourself are joining?"

"Yes, of course!" the Earl exclaimed.

"The Baron is only twenty-one," Captain Stanton went on. "As I expect you know already, David, a Knight cannot be in command of a ship until he is twenty-four and has done four 'caravans'."

There was no need to explain to Cordelia, who had heard her brother talk of it so often, that a 'caravan' was a cruise in the galleys, lasting at least six months.

These 'caravans' ensured that every Knight had experience of practical Naval matters, and had resulted in the Knights of Malta being recognised as the finest and most experienced Naval Captains in the world.

A Knight was not only a valiant fighter, dauntless and with a spirit of adventure which commanded admiration wherever he went, he was also so knowledgeable at sea that the Knights were greatly in demand as instructors.

"My ship, the *St. Jude*," Mark Stanton was explaining, "belongs to the Baron, and as the Order is at the moment short of vessels they welcome Knights who will provide their own."

"Perhaps that is something I can do later," the Earl said with glowing eyes.

"I see no reason why not, if you can afford it," his cousin answered.

"It is certainly an idea, and one that did not occur to me before," the Earl said. "When can I see your ship?"

"Any time you wish," Mark Stanton replied. "But as I have only just arrived here I would like, if you will allow me, to talk to you both for a little while before we go to the dock-yard."

"Yes – of course," David replied, while Cordelia with a smile explained :

"David dislikes Naples and is longing to reach Malta. He grudges every moment we must spend in this beautiful City."

"And you?" Mark Stanton asked.

"It is so lovely that I feel at times I must be dreaming!"

He sipped his wine before he said reflectively :

"When I want to think of somewhere lovely and peaceful I remember Stanton Park."

The Earl rose to his feet.

"I will go and get ready," he said, "so that when you are prepared to show me your ship I shall not keep you waiting."

"I am in no hurry," Mark Stanton answered.

The Earl however moved quickly across the polished floor with its expensive Persian rugs and Cordelia said with a smile :

"I am so glad you have come! David has been eating his heart out for fear that he would not reach Malta in the next few days."

Mark Stanton was still for a moment, then he said slowly:

"Have you really thought this over sensibly? David is not yet of age; is he wise to give up his English way of life?"

"I beg of you not to argue with him," Cordelia replied. "This has always been his vision, his dream, and nothing you or anyone else can say could dissuade him from the conviction that he has been called to the service of God in this special way."

Mark Stanton did not answer and after a moment she went on:

"I cannot tell you how nervous I was that he might not be accepted. It would have been a blow from which he would never have recovered."

"I see no reason why he should not have been accepted."

"We certainly have the requisite eight-quarterings to prove our nobility and the Stantons are a Catholic family. But I am sure that one of our relatives who lives in Rome was trying to persuade His Holiness the Pope to refuse David's application. In fact he more or less said so when he was in England."

"Have you any idea why he should do that?"

"He thought David was too young to know his own mind, and that he would doubtless fall in love and regret that he could not be married. I think he also resented so much of the Stanton fortune going to Malta."

"I should have thought those were all very strong and valid arguments," Mark Stanton remarked.

"It is not your place to try to interfere!" Cordelia retorted.

Even as she spoke she knew it sounded rude, but she had a feeling that she must protect her brother from this large, somehow overwhelming cousin.

She did not know why she felt that way, except that she remembered Mark had always upset her when she was a child.

He had teased her, and since he was so much older she

had been a little afraid of him. What was more, she admitted to herself, she had been jealous.

David, two years her senior, had been a close companion and she had imagined he was happy in her company when he was home from school.

The moment Mark appeared however he had run after him, fagged for him, and found his company infinitely preferable to that of his small sister.

"I think I have every right to try to stop David doing this," Mark said. "In fact I am the one person who should do it."

"Why should you think that?" Cordelia asked and now there was no doubt of the hostility in her voice.

"Quite simply because I am his heir!"

Cordelia looked at her cousin in a startled fashion.

"Are you? I did not realise that?"

"Unless David marries and has a son," he replied, "I shall on his death inherit the title. A very unlikely contingency, seeing that I am eight years older than he is."

He paused, then went on:

"At the same time, although undoubtedly I would be defrauding my son, if I ever have one, I consider that I should point out to David the disadvantages of his becoming a Knight of St. John."

Cordelia rose to her feet.

"I beg of you to do nothing of the sort. David has suffered quite enough criticism and opposition, and interference by people who quite frankly should mind their own business!"

"Which of course includes me?"

"We did not expect to find you here," Cordelia said. "It is just by chance that you should have come into Naples at this moment and be the Captain of a ship which is proceeding to Malta. All I can beg is that you will carry us as if we were ordinary passengers, not relatives."

"You know that is impossible," Mark Stanton replied. "Quite frankly, Cordelia, I am delighted to have such distinguished passengers and, may I say, one such lovely relative."

"And yet, you intend to harass David and make him unhappy?"

Mark Stanton rose slowly to his feet. There was, Cordelia thought, an athletic litheness about him that she would not have expected in such a big man.

"Let us talk about this coolly and sensibly," he suggested. "Does David believe he will be able to withstand the temptations of the flesh for the rest of his life?"

He was being cynical, Cordelia thought, and she replied hotly:

"Some men can find something better to do than to pursue, as the Neapolitans do, every pretty face they see!"

"Most Englishmen as it happens, are more discriminating," Mark Stanton smiled.

She knew he was laughing at her and hated him for it.

She remembered how he teased her for having a freckled nose when she was a child, and how there was always something about him that had made her feel small, insignificant and unsure of herself.

"You are to leave David alone!" she said angrily.

She knew even as she spoke that it was the wrong approach.

Young though she was and ignorant of the world, she knew instantly that to give orders to a man of Captain Stanton's calibre was to get nowhere.

But there was something about him which made her angry as it always had, and now because she felt she was making no impression on him she stamped her foot.

"Oh, do go away!" she cried. "The last thing either David or I require at this moment is a fault-finding relative. Forget you have come here and let us find another ship."

"You are not very complimentary Cordelia!" Mark Stanton said. "At the same time I cannot help feeling that your anger comes not so much from anything I have said, but simply because your common sense – or do you call it your conscience? – tells you that I am right?"

"It tells me nothing of the sort!" Cordelia snapped. "I want David to be happy. I know that is possible only if he is true to his ideals, if he dedicates himself as he wishes to do, to his faith."

To her surprise Mark Stanton did not reply immediately.

Instead he walked across the Salon to stand with his back to her, contemplating a portrait of Lady Hamilton painted by Madame Le Brun when she first came to Naples.

In her favourite 'attitude' of Bacchante she looked very lovely and there was something very young and very vulnerable about her which reminded him of Cordelia.

Watching him Cordelia felt somehow helpless and ineffective. He was so sure of himself, so determined, and, she thought, ruthless.

He turned from the picture to walk back to her.

"We have talked a great deal about David," he said. "Now tell me a little about yourself."

"What do you want to know?" Cordelia asked and there was no disguising the hostility in her voice.

"Let me put it quite clearly," Mark Stanton replied. "If David is to become a Knight of St. John, what will you do? As things are in the Mediterranean at the moment it may not be easy for you to get back to England."

"What do you mean by that exactly?"

"There is an obstacle of whom you may have heard called Napoleon Bonaparte," Mark Stanton replied sarcastically.

"I understood his Fleet is shut up in Toulon and blockaded by the British."

"And I hope they will remain there," he said, "but it is still a long and arduous journey from here to England."

"I ... I may not ... return to England."

"You mean there is someone here you might marry?"

"No ... no, of course ... not!" she said quickly.

"I cannot believe that Lady Hamilton has asked you to be her guest indefinitely."

He did not add, although he thought it, that Emma Hamilton would find a young and very beautiful woman an unwelcome rival for any length of time.

"No ... there is no one I would ... marry!" Cordelia murmured.

"Then what are your plans?"

"They are my own!"

"I think, as your nearest relative, in fact your only relative in this part of the world, that I have a right to be told them."

She wanted to refuse and he was aware of the conflict within her before she said, almost as if she were goaded into a reply:

"David has suggested that I ... enter the Convent of St. Romanica!"

"He has suggested *what*?"

The question seemed to vibrate around the Salon almost like a pistol shot.

"I ... am ... considering it," Cordelia said with dignity.

"Have the Stantons all gone crazy?" Mark Stanton ejaculated.

Now there was no doubt that he had been jolted out of the calm, cynical amusement with which he had regarded his cousins since he first arrived.

"It is bad enough," he went on, "that David should take vows he may bitterly regret later in his life; but that you should enter a convent at eighteen, having seen nothing of the world and looking as you do, is sheer unprecedented madness!"

There was so much anger in his tone that however much she tried to tell herself it was nothing to do with him, Cordelia felt afraid.

"I have said I am ... considering it," she said in a very small voice. "It is what David ... wants."

"There is something in the Stanton character," Mark Stanton said, "which makes them want to convert or proselytise others to their own way of thinking."

The anger abated in his voice a little as he went on:

"We have a joint Great-Uncle, or grandfather, I cannot remember which, who was a drunkard and invariably pestered his friends to get drunk with him. Another who was a gambler who infected with his vice the young men when they first arrived in Whites Club to such an extent that the majority of them were bankrupt within a few months."

"The examples you quote are hardly comparable," Cordelia said coldly.

"On the contrary, it is just the same idea! David wants to be a monk – you should become a nun. David wants to dedicate his life to some high and noble ideal – you must do like-

24

wise, regardless of whether it is a whole-hearted desire on your part to segregate yourself from the world."

Cordelia did not answer and after a moment he said angrily:

"Good God, Child, you have the whole of your life before you – a life that should be full and interesting, a life in which you will meet many men, who will fall in love with you and whom you may love in return."

Cordelia made a gesture as if she repudiated such an idea, but she did not speak and he went on:

"Can you really contemplate an existence of being shut up behind high walls, of living permanently and exclusively in the company of your own sex, a number of whom I am prepared to swear are not saintly, but aggressively feminine?"

Cordelia drew a deep breath.

"What I do or do not decide, Mark, it is for me to make the decision, and nothing you can do or say can stop me."

There was a moment's silence, then Mark Stanton said slowly:

"I am not so sure about that!"

"What do you mean?"

"I am thinking," he answered, "that I may be only your second or is it third cousin? Nevertheless, we are away from England, out of reach of older and nearer members of the family. I should imagine that in a Court of Law I would have a good claim to be appointed as your guardian!"

"David is my guardian since Papa died!" Cordelia said sharply.

"But David will be a Knight, and unless I am mistaken he will not be twenty-one for some months?"

"I do not know what you are contemplating," Cordelia said, "but whatever it is, will you please forget it? I will not acknowledge you are my guardian or as one who has the least authority over me."

She felt he was not impressed and went on angrily:

"I shall do as I wish to do, and what I consider best for myself. Anything you say either to me or to David will be just a waste of breath!"

Mark Stanton did not answer and again Cordelia stamped her foot.

"I hate you, Mark! I have always hated you! Go away and leave us alone! I was happy ... very happy until you came here!"

She turned her face away so that he should not see there were tears in her eyes. Then, although she had not heard him move, suddenly he was behind her and his hands were on her shoulders turning her round to face him.

"I am sorry, Cordelia," he said quietly. "I can see I have gone about this the wrong way. Will you forgive me?"

She was so astonished at his change of attitude and by the beguiling note in his voice that she stared at him wide-eyed.

Then he smiled. It was a smile, although she did not know it, that a great number of women had found irresistible, and he lifted her hand to his lips.

"Forgive me, Cordelia," he said again and kissed it.

She stood looking at him bewildered and taken off her guard because this was the last thing she had expected.

"Suppose you go and find David?" he suggested. "Then I will take you to see my ship. I will not be in the least surprised if David galvanises the indolent Neapolitans into working a great deal faster than they intend to do."

He was still holding her hand. Cordelia looked into his eyes and found it difficult to know what to say.

She was still seething with the anger he had aroused in her, and yet at the same time she found it hard, when he was so near, to go on raging at him.

Finally she pulled her fingers from his and hurried towards the door.

Only as she went towards her own bed-room was she conscious that the warm pressure of his mouth still lingered on her skin.

*   *   *

The Salon was bright with lights. They even shone amongst the flowers on the terrace, and the noise and laughter of voices seemed to ripple out from the windows into the soft velvet of the night.

There was the tinkle of mandolins and guitars and a soft breeze blew from the sea which relieved the heat of the day.

The smart carriages with their liveried lackeys set down an endless stream of elegant and be-jewelled guests at the Palazzo Sessa.

Men with their dark curls heavily powdered, and wearing an inordinate amount of decorations, were a colourful complement to women in silks, satins, gauzes and laces, glittering with jewellery which might have come from the fire of Vesuvius itself!

Among the chattering, gossiping crowd, Captain Stanton, who was a head taller than any other man present, looked with his unpowdered hair and sunburnt face like a giant among pygmies.

Cordelia, doing her best to avoid him, found it difficult not to find herself seeing him every time she looked amongst the Ambassador's guests.

Mark Stanton was well aware that the Neapolitans were proud, patriotic, intelligent and cultured.

In their ranks were many brilliant men, philosophers, scholars, writers and scientists, who loathed the reckless, heartless tyranny under which they lived.

They detested the Bourbon Royals, the meddling Austrian Queen with her secret police and her lazy, uncultured husband.

These were people, he was thinking as he moved among them, who would welcome an invasion by the French, and if it came to the point of war, would undoubtedly put up very little resistance, if any, against Napoleon.

Because however he had frequently been to Naples he was well aware that the one bulwark against the French designs was Queen Marie Carolina.

Since her sister Marie Antoinette had been executed in Paris, the Queen had loathed the French with a hatred that was pathological.

Her closest friend, confidante, guide and adviser was undoubtedly the wife of the British Ambassador, the beautiful Emma Hamilton who, because of her humble origin, was rated of no consequence at all in England.

Mark Stanton knew that, when the French Fleet under Admiral La Touche had put into Naples, not only did the war-ships of France over-awe the populace, but also the guns of the French Fleet had been pointed at the City.

King Ferdinand had been given one hour in which to decide whether they should be fired or not.

Flabby with fright the King had accepted terms of abject submission in his painted cabinet, but when the ponderous ships had moved slowly down the Bay there were many Neapolitans who watched the departure of the tricolour with regret.

It remained to be seen, Mark Stanton thought, what would happen if the English Fleet came to Malta.

Would Queen Marie Carolina and Lady Hamilton be strong enough to defy the King and victual the British ships?

However nothing of what he was thinking showed in his face as he smiled at the beautiful women who were trying flirtatiously to attract his attention, and answered respectfully the Neapolitan Statesmen who considered him nothing but an adventurous Corsair.

Late in the evening he realised that he had not seen Cordelia for some time and thought, because it was so hot in the Salon, he might find her in the garden.

There was no sign of her on the terrace and he moved through the orange, lemon and pomegranate trees, seeing the fire-flies dancing among the blossoms and watching for a moment the lanterns of pleasure-boats glinting beyond the shipping in the quiet Bay.

He had a sudden longing to be away from the glittering throng and down on the crowded Quayside, where the fisherfolk lounged and gossiped wearing striped trousers and red jackets, black caps and gold ear-rings.

There their voices would be raised in song and every shadowy corner would be filled with a man and a woman locked in each other's arms.

It would be gay, it would be natural, and to Mark Stanton at this moment preferable in every way to the perfumed artificial pretensions of the guests around him.

To a great number of them, he knew, he was an enemy,

the representative of a country which was opposing Bonaparte in his fevered impatience to have all Europe beneath
his heel.

He still had not found Cordelia and he moved further
down the garden, wondering if she had been enticed by
some amorous young aristocrat into such a romantic setting.

Then suddenly as he stood alone she was beside him, and
even before her hands went out to clasp his arm he knew
with an unmistakable instinct that she was frightened.

"I ... I saw that y.you were ... a.alone," she stam-
mered.

"What has happened?" he enquired. "Who has upset
you?"

He could see her face very clearly not only in the light
from a lantern hanging in the bough of one of the trees, but
also in the light from the stars which made the whole sky a
glittering panorama of indescribable beauty.

"I am ... all right ... now."

She was not stammering and yet he knew her breath was
coming quickly from between her parted lips and her small
breasts were stirring tumultuously against the bodice of her
low cut gown.

"Tell me what has frightened you," Mark Stanton insisted.

"It is ... foolish of me, but ..."

Her voice died away and he had the feeling she was trying to decide whether she should trust him or not.

He did not move, merely waited, and to Cordelia his very
presence was somehow comforting and gave her a sense of
security.

He was so big, so strong, and he was English. He was also
her cousin.

She made up her mind.

"Please ... Mark ... will you ... help me?"

Chapter Two

"Why must you leave so soon?"

The voice, low and a little tired but caressing, came from the bed. Mark Stanton looked towards the first rays of sunshine coming through the open windows and replied:

"I dislike arriving back at my lodgings in full evening dress when the sun is up."

"The Neapolitans think it proves their virility!"

There was a soft laugh.

"But you, my Man of the Sea, have no need to prove yours!"

Mark Stanton turned to smile at the speaker, his strong athletic body silhouetted against the mirrors on the dressing-table with its profusion of lotions, creams and salves glittering on its painted surface.

From her pillows Princess Gianetta di Sapuano watched him with smouldering velvet black eyes which no man as experienced in women as Mark Stanton could mistake.

Her hair, which was like silk to his touch, held strange purple lights in its darkness as it fell over the lace-edged pillows.

Her parted lips were red and inviting in an oval face to which poets had written odes and which artists had tried vainly to reproduce on canvas.

At twenty-six Princess Gianetta was at the height of her beauty.

There was no-one in the whole of Naples who could rival either her sensational attractions or the position she held in that snob-ridden, class-conscious society.

Widowed before she was twenty-one, the Princess had refused all further offers of marriage and preferred to choose her lovers with discrimination while enjoying the freedom which her late husband's enormous fortune ensured for her.

Every time he came to Naples, Mark Stanton visited her, and he was well aware that he was regarded by her other admirers with a jealousy which at times was almost murderous!

"I was hoping you would not be away for long," the Princess said now, "and it was like an answer to prayer when I saw you at the British Embassy this evening."

"I knew you would be there," Mark Stanton replied.

He fastened his fine linen shirt deftly, with the ease of a man who was used to dressing himself without the help of a valet.

There was silence in the bed-room scented with a fragrance which all the Princess's lovers associated only with her.

It was distinctive, unusual and had a persistent, haunting aroma which remained on their hands, their bodies and in their nostrils long after they had left her bed.

There were great bowls of flowers on the balcony outside the window, and the huge carved headboard of the bed and its draped curtains of jade green silk were a perfect frame for its owner's exotic beauty.

The Princess raised herself a little on the pillows regardless of the fact that the action revealed even more of her perfectly proportioned body and that her pink-tipped breasts were an invitation to the man watching her.

"Have you ever thought, Mark, of marriage?"

He picked up his well-cut evening-coat from the chair on which he had thrown it before he answered:

"Am I to take this, Gianetta *mia*, as a proposal?"

His eyes were twinkling and there was a note of amusement in his voice.

"Suppose it was one?"

The reply from the bed astonished him and he paused in the act of putting his arm into his coat-sleeve.

"If you are serious – you know the answer."

There was a little sigh.

"Yes, I know the answer. You want to be free to roam

31

about the world committing reckless acts of piracy which one day may prove fatal!"

"The alternative to being enclosed in a gilded cage! My dear Gianetta, you cannot confine a wild animal."

"Even the wildest, I am told, can be tamed."

Mark Stanton laughed.

"That is debatable, a fairy-story made up to instruct children in kindness towards dumb beasts."

The Princess suddenly put out her arms towards him.

"I want you, Mark! I want you!"

Now there was a note of passion in her voice that was unmistakable.

"Stay with me," she went on. "Stay with me at least as long as you are here in Naples. And when you leave, you will take my heart with you."

Mark Stanton pulled the lapels of his coat into place. Then he walked towards the bed to stand looking down at its alluring and very lovely occupant.

Gianetta was, he thought, one of the most beautiful women he had ever known. She was also one of the most passionate.

He lifted her hand from the sheet on which it lay and raised it to his lips.

"Thank you," he said gently, "for the happiness you have given me tonight and at other times."

She knew without words that he refused what she suggested. Yet because like all women she wished to have her own way, her fingers tightened on his.

"I said that I wanted you."

"You are insatiable!"

"Where you are concerned that is true. With other men I am the one who tires."

He released her hand and touched the shadows beneath her eyes.

"Go to sleep, Gianetta."

"I shall only dream of you."

"I wonder."

"That is true, and it would be much more satisfying if you were here when I woke."

· She threw back her head in a passionate gesture of surrender.

"No, Gianetta, I am leaving. I have a ship which is waiting for me."

His eyes were laughing but the Princess held on to him when he would have moved.

"Do not go yet," she begged. "We have not had time to talk and there is so much I want to ask you, so much I wish to hear."

"At this time in the morning?"

"Why not?" she enquired. "And if you will not talk of love, let us speak of the political situation."

Her fingers caressed his as she asked:

"With how many ships is Admiral Nelson blockading the French Fleet in Toulon?"

"You are interested?" Mark Stanton enquired.

"But of course! I have no wish to see the French in Naples again."

"And yet the French Resident would be extremely interested in the answer I might give to your question."

He felt her stiffen. Then as she peeped up at him a little apprehensively from under her long dark eye-lashes, he laughed.

"Gianetta, my sweet," he said affectionately, "you will never make a good spy, and you have so many other much more alluring talents."

Her eyes met his.

"The French Resident is so grateful for even a tiny piece of information."

"And I would of course be equally grateful for anything you might be able to tell me."

The Princess hesitated for a moment, then she said:

"Napoleon Bonaparte has been told that the Russians are interested in acquiring Malta."

Mark Stanton sat down on the bed.

"Tallyrand informed Bonaparte last year that Malta was a hive of Austrian, Russian and English spies."

"It is no secret that he, himself, provided two more, one Maltese, one French!"

Mark Stanton knew the Princess was listening, and went on :

"The Czar Paul has founded a Russian Priory of the Order of St. John. The only use he has for Malta is that the Grand Master should send him Knights to teach seamanship to Russian Officers."

His eyes were watching the expression on the Princess's face as he continued :

"I can assure you that the fortifications of Malta are impregnable if adequately defended ! And that is something you can tell the French Resident, so that he can pass it on to Bonaparte with all possible speed !"

There was something contemptuous in his tone and in reply the Princess put her arms around his neck and drew his lips down on hers.

"Forgive me," she said, "I should not have tried such an old trick to keep you interested and with me for a little while longer."

Her arms tightened as she whispered :

"Because you are English my sympathies are with your country-men and not with the French, but really I am interested in only one person – you !"

Her lips were pressed against his and Mark Stanton felt the passion in them.

He kissed her, then resolutely he unfastened her arms from around his neck and rose to his feet.

"Good-bye, most beguiling and unforgettable Gianetta."

"I shall see you again ?"

It was both a plea and a question.

"I am not certain when I will be leaving," he replied evasively.

"I love you ! Oh, Mark, remember that I love you !"

He smiled at her from the doorway. Then as her arms went out to him despairingly he was gone and the door shut behind him.

The Princess gave a little cry and threw herself back against the pillows, her face hidden in their soft silk.

Outside the Palazzo the air was fresh and there was that lucidity of light that was peculiar to Naples and had a brilliance which Mark Stanton had found nowhere else in the world.

Although it was still very early, the streets were full of people going to work, to Church, to the Quay! The majority of the women wore red skirts and white aprons, the men striped shirts, black caps and bright sashes.

There were the cheerful, insolent *lazzaroni*, the idle, jolly and picturesque fishermen, the trades people and the loungers who formed a large part of the population, all yawning after a night of insufficient sleep.

The bells were beginning to toll in the belfries and towers of the innumerable Churches, and women with lace veils over their heads were hurrying up the steps to Mass.

There were monks, nuns and Priests appearing from every direction.

Mark Stanton sauntered along with an air of superiority which made those he met invariably step out of his way to let him pass.

But he was thinking not of Gianetta, whose fragrance still lingered with him, but of Cordelia.

He could hear her voice as she had said: "Please . . . Mark . . . will you . . . help me?"

It was the cry of a child.

"Let us sit down somewhere where we can talk," he had said quietly.

Taking her by the hand he led her through the shrubs heavy with blossom to where there was a seat in an arbour overlooking the Bay.

Here they were shut off from the rest of the garden and the ground dropped beneath them so that they could look out towards the deep blue horizon where the sea met the starlit sky.

The arbour had been discreetly lit with a small lantern, by the light of which Mark Stanton, sitting sideways to look at Cordelia, could see the fear in her eyes.

As they sat down she had taken her hand from his and now she sat with her back straight, her head on its long neck held high, and yet there was something defenceless about her.

35

She stared straight ahead and Mark Stanton had the idea she was feeling for words.

"Tell me," he prompted gently.

"It is . . . the Duca di Belina," she said slowly after a moment.

Mark Stanton raised his eye-brows, but he did not speak and after a moment she went on :

"He . . . he will not . . . leave me alone. He has spoken to . . . Lady Hamilton, and she favours his . . . suit."

"He wishes to marry you?"

Cordelia nodded her head.

"He asked me to do so the second time we met . . . and although I . . . refused he will not take . . . no for an . . . answer."

"You have spoken about this to David?"

"Yes."

"And what did he say?"

"He thought it would be a very . . . advantageous marriage for me . . . Of course the Duca is looked upon as being very important in Naples."

"He is important!" Mark Stanton said. "But you do not like him?"

"I . . . hate him!" Cordelia replied. "I hate him and he . . . frightens me!"

She turned her head towards her cousin for the first time and she said with a throb of fear in her voice :

"You will think me . . . foolish. Like Lady Hamilton . . . you will perhaps press me to accept the Duca . . . but I . . . cannot."

"Why not?"

Cordelia hesitated for a moment, then she said in a very small voice :

"I do not . . . love him!"

"You consider love important?"

She put out her hands almost pleadingly towards him, then she dropped them.

"You will not . . . understand," she said, "I know you are thinking that I should be . . . grateful that anyone who belongs to such a . . . noble family, who is so rich and power-

36

ful and the owner of vast possessions, should wish to . . . marry me, but . . ."

She stopped and after a moment Mark Stanton asked curiously :

"What is the end of that sentence?"

". . . I could not . . . let him . . . touch me," Cordelia replied almost in a whisper.

"Then the Duca must accept that as final," Mark Stanton said.

"Will you make him do so?" she asked quickly. "Will you make him understand that I will not change my mind and that he must not come . . . near me . . . must not try to . . . kiss me . . . as he was . . . trying to do . . . just now."

"Is the Duca perhaps one of the reasons why you were thinking of entering a Convent?"

There was silence and once again Mark Stanton had the feeling that Cordelia was wondering whether she should trust him or not

"I want to understand everything," he said quietly.

"There was . . . another man in England before we left," Cordelia began after a moment. "He lives near Stanton Park and I have known him for some . . . years."

"He asked you to marry him?"

"Yes . . . and like the Duca he would not . . . listen to me. He called every day . . . he wrote . . . he spoke to . . . David."

She gave a deep sigh.

"It was all very . . . difficult."

"You were not in love with him?"

"No, he was horrible! There was something coarse and unpleasant about him. I cannot explain because he was very popular with both men and women, but I knew the face he showed to the world was not . . . really what he was . . . like inside."

"And what did David think about him?"

"He . . . wanted me to . . . marry him."

There was a pause, then Cordelia said :

"I can understand David's point of view. He wants me to settle down so that he can feel free to live his own life without his conscience pricking him where I am concerned."

37

"So to prevent that happening he has suggested that you should be incarcerated in a Convent!"

There was no mistaking the sarcasm and also the note of accusation in Mark Stanton's tone.

"Perhaps David is right in thinking that is . . . where I might find . . . happiness."

"I do not believe that."

"I have . . . thought," Cordelia said hesitatingly, "that there . . . might be something . . . wrong with me. Perhaps I am . . . different from other women in that I cannot . . . respond to the men who say they . . . love me."

She was twisting her fingers together as if to speak of what she felt inside herself was to reveal fears which were very real.

Mark Stanton bent forward and put his hand over hers.

"Listen to me, Cordelia," he said, "and listen attentively."

She was still at the touch of his fingers and now her eyes were raised to his obediently.

"There is nothing wrong in what you are feeling," he said. "You are not different from other women in any way except perhaps that you are more sensitive and your standards are higher than theirs."

"I do not . . . understand."

"I will try to put it into simple words," he said. "In every man and woman there is a dream, a vision if you like, for which they yearn and to which they aspire."

"Like David and his . . . longing to be a Knight?"

"Exactly!" Mark Stanton agreed. "But for most of us it is very much more simple. We seek love and we try to find it with someone of the opposite sex."

"But love . . ." Cordelia began and stopped.

He knew she was thinking of the love which she had seen since she came to Naples.

The amorous voices and the unceasing flirtations of the Neapolitans, the pursuit of women which was the sport of Italian Princelings and young Patricians.

Deceiving wives, unfaithful husbands, and barely veiled indiscretions were all a part of every Neapolitan's way of life.

"What you see here is not love," Mark Stanton said harshly. "Not love as I am speaking of it, not the love you are seeking, Cordelia."

He felt as if she moved a little closer to him as she said :

"Explain it to . . . me so that I can . . . understand."

"Love is divine and comes from a power beyond ourselves," he said, "but because people cannot always find the real thing; rather than lack love altogether they put up with the imitation, the second rate, the common-place."

"And that it what is . . . happening here?"

"To the Neapolitans love and the idea of being in love are as natural as the air they breathe," Mark Stanton said. "They are a passionate, emotional, warm-hearted people."

"I know . . . that."

"But for those of us who come from a colder and more austere climate love is not so simple. Yet, if we find it, because we love not only with our hearts and bodies, but also with our minds and souls, it is much more wonderful."

He paused to say very quietly :

"In fact it can be the dream we are all seeking and which lies in a secret shrine within ourselves."

Cordelia gave a little cry.

"Now I understand! Now I know . . . that is what I want . . . what I have always wanted."

She looked at Mark Stanton and her eyes were very large in her small face.

"Suppose I never . . . find it?"

Again there was a touch of fear in her voice, but this time it was different.

"Will you trust me," he said, "when I promise you that you will find love? The love in which you believe, the love that you are sure of in your heart, but which has not yet come into your life."

"I want to believe it will . . . happen."

"It will!" Mark Stanton said confidently.

Cordelia gave a little sigh.

"You have made everything seem so simple and I am no longer frightened about myself."

"I want you to promise me something."

She looked at him a little apprehensively.

"I want you to promise," he said, "that you will give life a chance, ordinary life as you and I live it, before you do anything drastic."

"You mean such as . . . going into a . . . Convent?" Cordelia asked.

"I mean also in not agreeing to marry any man unless you are completely and absolutely certain that the love he offers you and the love you can give him are the real and genuine love you are seeking in your dream."

"I promise!" Cordelia said.

There was a smile on her lips for the first time since they had been talking together. Then she added quickly:

"You will speak to the . . . Duca?"

"I will deal with the Duca," Mark Stanton said firmly. "He will not trouble you again, Cordelia, and you can send any other importunate Beau to me. I am quite prepared to listen to the eulogies of your attractions, then kick him downstairs!"

Cordelia looked startled.

"I would not wish you to be unnecessarily harsh with anyone," she said. "After all, I suppose it is a compliment that they want me?"

"Not in every case," Mark Stanton replied. "Do not trouble your head over it any more, Cordelia. As long as we are in Naples I will look after you."

"And when we are in . . . Malta?" Cordelia murmured.

"I do not expect I shall be far away."

He rose to his feet.

"I am taking you back to the Ball-Room. As I have now constituted myself your guardian I cannot allow you to stay too long in the garden. If people notice your absence they might find a wrong explanation for your being away so long."

He knew by the expression on Cordelia's face that this was something that had never occurred to her.

"Should I not have gone into the garden?" she asked.

"It was not very wise unless you were willing to find

yourself in the uncomfortable situation which you experienced when alone with the Duca."

"It was . . . foolish of me," Cordelia admitted, "but he was so . . . insistent, and I did not know how to . . . refuse."

"Another time be quite firm in saying No," Mark Stanton ordered with a smile.

"I will do that."

They had moved to where the path led from the arbour, and now she stopped still and the light from the stars turned her hair to a silvery gold.

"Thank you," she said softly. "I am sorry I was . . . rude to you to-day, but you . . . frightened me."

"And now?" Mark Stanton enquired.

"I am no longer afraid, and . . . I trust you."

She looked up at him.

He was very tall and strong and she felt glad he was her cousin and she need no longer be afraid.

To Mark Stanton she appeared very ethereal in her white gown; she seemed to merge with the flowers around her, with the stars which shone above, and the sea which glittered below.

She was a part of them, and yet she was distinctly and individually herself.

'She is like a snow-drop,' he thought suddenly.

For a moment the over-scented, lush Italian night vanished and he saw instead the Park at Stanton and the snow-drops, white and pure, pushing their way through the snow beneath the high oak trees.

"A snow-drop!" Mark Stanton repeated now as he walked homewards.

He knew that Cordelia was just as fragile, as delicate and as sensitive as the first flower of an English spring.

* * *

In the Palazzo Sessa Cordelia awoke when the sun was golden over the city and was aware of a new happiness that she had not felt for a long time.

She felt secure and protected.

It was something which she had lost when her father

died, but which, magically, Mark Stanton had brought back to her so that she was no longer unsure and apprehensive.

"He was kind," she told herself, "far kinder than I ever imagined he could be!"

Then she wondered if he had been bored with talking to her for so long, and whether he found her very stupid and dull beside the entertaining, glittering ladies she had seen surrounding him the whole evening.

There was one in particular who she had thought was the most beautiful woman she had ever seen.

She had in fact met her before Mark's arrival and knew she was the Princess Gianetta di Sapuano.

She was a frequent visitor at the British Embassy and at every party Cordelia attended she was the most outstanding woman present, so that everyone seemed to gravitate towards her like moths to a lantern.

'She is very beautiful!' Cordelia thought and felt that in contrast her own pale gold hair and white skin were insipid.

She remembered now that when they had gone back into the Salon where the Band was playing soft romantic music they had hardly stepped from the terrace before the Princess had moved towards Mark Stanton.

"I was half-afraid you had vanished!" she said in a possessive tone that had a note of passion in it, that was unmistakable.

It was impossible for Cordelia not to notice too the manner in which her eyes looked provocatively at Mark Stanton and her lips parted invitingly.

She had never imagined that a woman could look so voluptuous and at the same time so genuinely beautiful.

She found herself thinking of the Sirens who had sung to Ulysses, who had only been able to escape their fatal charms by plugging his sailors' ears with wax and having himself tied fast to the mast.

There was, Cordelia thought, something in the Princess's voice that was irresistible.

Perhaps it was her slight accent which made her English sound so much more interesting and attractive than when it was spoken by an Englishwoman.

Perhaps it was because she seemed to speak to Mark Stanton differently to the way in which she spoke to anyone else.

The partner whose dance Cordelia had forgotten and who reproached her for her neglect, now claimed her.

When she had finished dancing with him, she realised that she could no longer see her cousin, Mark, in the Salon, and the Princess also appeared to be missing.

*   *   *

When she was dressed Cordelia went downstairs to find David just coming in through the front door.

"You are up early, dearest!" she exclaimed. "Where have you been?"

"I have been to the dock-yard," he answered. "Mark gave me permission yesterday to spur on those lazy workmen, and that is exactly what I have been doing."

"When do you think the ship will be ready?"

David made an expressive gesture with his hands, a trick he had picked up from the Neapolitans.

"Heaven knows!" he answered. "They have no intention of hurrying themselves. There is always some excuse for their negligence."

"You will have to possess your soul in patience!" Cordelia laughed. "And after all, David, it is only fair that after a long cruise Mark, and of course the owner, should have a little relaxation."

David's eyes seemed to light up.

"We are to meet the Baron to-day," he said. "He is staying with friends outside Naples, but I understand Sir William has invited him to luncheon."

"Sir William has been so kind," Cordelia said. "I think, David, it would seem rather ungrateful if you expressed too openly in his presence your fervent desire to depart from Naples."

"But that is exactly what I do want! I cannot bear to sit about here doing nothing when I might be with the Knights."

"It cannot be very long now," Cordelia said consolingly.

They walked out onto the terrace and after the cool of the Salon the sun was almost blinding.

"Every day will seem like a century until I reach Malta," David said. "Besides, I am afraid something might stop us."

"What do you mean by 'something'?" Cordelia enquired.

David glanced over his shoulder as if he was afraid of being overheard.

"Everyone was talking last night of the enormous fleet Bonaparte is preparing in Toulon. Some people think he has a secret plan."

"It is quite obvious," Cordelia answered, "that if he has superiority in ships, he is hoping to escape the watch of the British! He may be planning some new campaign by sea."

"Why should he wish to move? – that is the point!" David said. "There is plenty for him to conquer without leaving dry land."

"More fighting, more suffering! How I hate war!" Cordelia exclaimed.

"All women feel the same," David replied. "At the same time I cannot help thinking that Bonaparte is rather fantastic."

"Fantastic?"

"Do you realise," David asked, "in a simple campaign he has defeated five armies, won eighteen pitched battles and sixty-seven smaller combats? He has taken one hundred and fifty thousand prisoners!"

He paused to add impressively:

"Sir William reckons he has added two hundred million francs to the Treasury of France."

"He has not yet conquered England, nor is he likely to!" Cordelia exclaimed hotly.

"Nor would he ever be able to conquer Malta," David said with a note of elation in his voice. "Do you remember, Cordelia, how I read to you the story of the Siege by the Turks – the most famous Siege in history?"

"That took place a long time ago."

"In 1565," David supplied, "and never had there been such bravery, such endurance, such amazing courage, as the Knights showed."

His voice rang out as he went on:

"The Knights saved Sicily and Southern Italy from the Turks. They were out-gunned and out-manned, but they won!"

"You have told me about it so often," Cordelia said gently.

"Who knows when we may have to fight again?" David went on. "Even if it is against the whole might of the French Fleet I know, Cordelia, we will win!"

"Of course you will, dearest," Cordelia said, anxious to agree with him. "Malta is the strongest fortified place in the whole world."

"Fortifications are no use without the right men to man them."

There was a sudden light in David's eyes and a note of elation in his voice as he cried:

"If only I could have the chance to prove myself! If only I could fight like Jean de la Valette during the Siege and carry the Cross to victory!"

Cordelia walked up to her brother and putting her arms on his shoulders kissed his cheek.

"I know that whatever happens you will always do what is right, and noble," she said. "But, oh, David, I am afraid when I think of you fighting!"

"I want to fight for my faith," David answered, "but I assure you that I intend to be an expert swordsman and a first class shot!"

"You are that anyway," Cordelia said quickly.

"I hope so," he replied, "but shooting at partridges is rather different from aiming at men."

Cordelia shuddered.

"I do not like to think of you killing anyone, David, even if they are not Christians."

She could not help wondering as she spoke how many people who professed the Christian faith carried out any of its tenets.

The Churches in Naples might be full, but she was well aware that much of the great and powerful religion to which she belonged had sunk into gross superstitions that were shared alike by the Queen and the beggars.

All Neapolitans feared the *iettatura* or Evil Eye, and protected themselves by touching a little bone or coral horn they carried in their pockets.

When she had been in Naples a few days she had been taken to the Cathedral where amid scenes of almost frantic excitement the Bishop had shown the phial in which the blood of the Patron Saint of Naples, Saint Gennaro, was changed from a solidified drop into a fresh crimson liquid.

While Cordelia had been prepared to believe in the miracle, she had in fact felt a distaste she could not check for the hysterical emotionalism of the worshippers.

They had been so unrestrained, so carried away by the ceremony which occurred every year, that some critical part of her mind felt their behaviour was unnatural.

It would be better, she thought, to show more kindliness and charity to their fellow-beings.

Outside the beggars with their sores, their rags, their blind eyes and their stunted limbs were a disgrace to any civilised country.

But she was well aware that little or nothing was done for them and she had been told that the hospitals were inadequate because there was not enough money to help those who clamoured for attention and were in desperate need of treatment.

She tried not to find fault, just as she tried to understand her brother David's longing to reach Malta where all his dreams would come true.

While they were still on the terrace Lady Hamilton came through the open windows to join them.

She was looking very lovely and her face even in the brilliance of the sun had a beauty that the most famous artists could not depict in their paintings.

"Good-morning, my dears!"

She greeted them in her gay voice which occasionally, despite all her lessons, had when she spoke in English, an uncultured note in it.

Cordelia curtsied while David raised his hostess's hand to his lips.

"Good-morning, My Lady!"

"Did you enjoy yourself last night – you naughty boy!"
Lady Hamilton enquired. "I saw you slip away at almost
the beginning of the party. Where did you hide yourself?"

"I had some books to read and some prayers to say,"
David said quite simply.

Lady Hamilton smiled at him and there was a softness in
her eyes as she remarked:

"So young and so ardent! As I said to Sir William last
night, no-one could be better cast for the part of a perfect
and gentle Knight."

David flushed, but Cordelia could see that he was pleased
with the compliment.

Lady Hamilton turned towards her.

"And you, Cordelia, you were a great success, and very
greatly admired!"

She paused to say a little archly:

"And by one person in particular!"

Cordelia did not answer and after a moment she went on:

"The Duca di Belina is very much in love with you. Do not
keep him waiting too long for his answer. It would be a mistake to lose him."

"The Duca has had my answer," Cordelia said quietly.

"My dear child, you mean . . ."

"I have refused to marry him, My Lady, but he will not
take no for an answer. So I have asked my cousin to speak
to him."

"Captain Stanton?" Lady Hamilton queried.

Then she laughed.

"Has Mark Stanton assumed such responsibilities?"

She laughed again.

"I cannot quite see him in the position of *Paterfamilias*.
He has always been a Don Juan or Casanova who has kissed
and run away, leaving a trail of broken hearts behind him!"

Cordelia looked startled.

"I cannot imagine Cousin Mark being like that."

"Perhaps you see him through different eyes," Lady
Hamilton replied. "Or perhaps you should ask the alluring
Princess Gianetta di Sapuano what she feels about him!"

"The Princess?"

"She adores your cousin, and he her!" Lady Hamilton said. "I can assure you it is the *on dit* of Naples and has been for some years."

She gave a little sigh.

"They are both extremely handsome and will suit each other. I feel quite envious of them!"

As she spoke Lady Hamilton moved back into the Salon where a servant had appeared with a note which he carried on a silver salver.

Cordelia's eyes followed her. At the same time she was thinking in consternation of what she had just heard.

"Cousin Mark and the Princess Gianetta!"

Somehow, she thought, she might have suspected it last night when they had come in from the garden and the Princess had behaved so possessively towards him.

She did not know why – after all it was not her concern – but she felt upset at the thought of Mark marrying the beautiful Neapolitan Princess.

Would he be prepared to leave the sea? To live in Naples?

She could not imagine him in such a foreign environment. He had always seemed to belong to England, to Stanton, where he had fished in the lake, ridden over the broad acres and shot partridge, pheasant and snipe.

She could remember him coming in wet and muddy from hunting, throwing himself down in front of a log fire while a valet removed his riding-boots.

She could see him coming into the Nursery when she was just about to go to bed, resplendent in his evening clothes and looking very adult and grown up, while she was drinking her milk, wearing the nightgown which Nanny had warmed on the guard in front of the fire.

Looking back now she realised that Mark had been very much a part of her childhood, so much so that now he seemed since last night to have stepped back into the position he had held then of being one of her family.

She may have been angry with him, she may have been jealous, she may at times have even disliked him.

But he had been there, just as David was there, a Stanton, someone who belonged, and for whom therefore she had a more intimate feeling than she could feel for anyone else.

But Mark and the Princess!

She did not understand why it upset her or why the sun seemed somehow less golden than it had before.

*   *   *

Mark Stanton, reaching the dock-yard after luncheon, found, as he expected, the workmen having their inevitable siesta, and David tramping about trying to find someone who would listen to his pleas that they should return to work.

Mark laughed at him.

"My dear David, if you could change the habits of the Neapolitans you would be the greatest commander of men the world has ever known! Nothing and nobody could prevent them sleeping at this time of day, but they start early and they work late."

"Will this ship ever be repaired?" David enquired.

"It will be done in good time, and done well! Is Ludwig with you?"

"He is down below," David replied. "He feels as frustrated as I do."

"I am glad you have met."

David smiled and for the moment he seemed to forget his frustration.

"I think the Baron is absolutely charming!" he said. "He has been telling me lots of things I wanted to know. It is extremely fortunate that I met him before I arrived at my Auberge or I might have made a dozen mistakes!"

Mark Stanton thought the same thing and he was quite sure that the rather shy but charming young Bavarian would get on well with David.

There was no doubt later that the two young men were destined to be great friends.

Already it was obvious that they laughed at the same jokes, shared the same interests and behaved, Mark Stanton thought to himself, very much like two undergraduates during their first term at a University.

And after all that was exactly what the Order of St. John was to the young Knights, who were naturally at that age full of high spirits and irrepressible.

There would be plenty of time, Mark Stanton thought philosophically, for David to find that life was not quite so serious as he envisaged it, and that high spirits and a certain amount of horse-play were all part of life in Malta.

One of the great difficulties for a Knight was to find enough to do.

With its restricted size and limited resources the island was not really large enough for the number of hot-blooded proud young men who were thrown together into the communal life.

High spirits sometimes initiated a rag which degenerated into violence. Often some real or pretended insult to their dignity would bring the young aristocrats into open revolt.

"Discipline," some of the older Knights had said to Mark Stanton often enough, "is a major problem."

There were a great number of punishments for Knights who were disobedient or who broke the rules, but under the New Grand Master these were not so strictly applied as they had been under Emmanual de Rohan.

The Prince had been one of the finest Grand Masters the Order had ever known, but he had died the previous year.

The present Grand Master, Ferdinard von Hompesch, was only fifty-four and he had neither the strength of character nor the authority that was required for such an important position.

Mark Stanton would not have mentioned it either to David or to Ludwig von Wütenstein, but he was apprehensive in view of the many rumours regarding Napoleon's strategy in the Mediterranean as to whether von Hompesch was ready to ensure that Malta maintained her Sovereignty.

This was however only a secret apprehension at the back of his mind.

He had the greatest admiration for Malta and for its Knights, and he was well aware that every year the Grand Master's position became more difficult and more vulnerable.

One of the most unpleasant shocks the Order had received was when, after the Revolution in France and the execution of Louis XVI, all the possessions of the Knights in France had been confiscated.

This meant that the Grand Master, Emmanual de Rohan, had died a poor man.

What was more, even before his death, the temporal power of Malta had already seriously waned.

The opposition of Rome, the interference of Naples, and the abandonment by France had defeated him.

The times were against him, and Mark Stanton could not help asking himself whether time was not against the Order itself.

The Knights with their magnificent and glorious history might be facing a situation in which they would no longer be able to survive.

Then he heard the laughing voices of David and the young Baron coming up the companionway onto the deck and told himself that he was being unnecessarily apprehensive.

There were still young men from every country in Europe ready to live and if necessary die for their faith.

They still believed in the great ideals which had echoed down the centuries like a trumpet-call to the adventurous, the courageous and the gallant.

As long as that spirit continued, nothing could destroy the power of the Eight-Pointed Cross!

Chapter Three

Cordelia walked onto the terrace to look out over the Bay.

To-morrow they were leaving and she could hardly bear to think that she might never see the beauty of Naples again.

She felt as if she must imprint on her mind the whole wonder of it, so that it would be with her for ever, wherever she might be.

Was there anywhere else in the world, she asked herself, where the light was so translucent that it seemed as if it came from the gods themselves?

There was beauty everywhere.

From the sloping hills where the Convents blazed white beneath their belfries to the arcades in the city, where pots of camellias, red, white and striped, grew beside the statues of ancient gods.

She looked up to where the sombre splendour of Vesuvius rising from the fields of lava and ashes was smoking against the clear blue of the sky.

Amid the peaceful loveliness it struck a discordant note of danger, and to Cordelia it suggested there might be an eruption from the mountain or something even more explosive nearer at hand.

But her mind shied away from politics and the tension which always existed beneath the laughter and the false gaiety of Naples.

To-day she wanted only to think of the flowers, and instinctively she left the terrace to walk into the garden amidst the fragrant petals of the blossoming shrubs.

As she moved she disturbed a profusion of colourful butterflies who with the bees were hovering over the open blooms.

Far away in the distance, so faint it was only a whisper on the air, she could hear someone singing *Santa Lucia*, the song that was so much a part of Naples that it almost took the place of the National Anthem.

Mingling with the song of the birds it satisfied her hearing, as the loveliness around her satisfied her sight.

That the ship was finished and they could leave very early to-morrow morning was news which had sent David into ecstasies.

Without enquiring for him Cordelia was sure that he and the Baron would have gone down to the dock-yard first thing this morning.

The two young men would wish to assist in victualling the ship for the voyage, seeing that the water-butts were filled, and attending to the thousand and one things which had to be inspected before they could depart.

It was still very early and Lady Hamilton was asleep, while Sir William was doubtless attending to the many callers who started arriving at the Embassy first thing in the morning.

It was a relief to think that she could be alone.

She could not help thinking in retrospect that far too much of her visit to this enchanted City had been spent in parties and in the company of people with whom she had very little in common.

Cordelia was used to being on her own, because at Stanton Park when David had been at school or at his University she had no companionship except for her teachers.

She would wander in the gardens and in the Park, not lonely, but content with her own company and the resourcefulness of her imagination.

She had in fact invented a fantasy world from the stories she had read of mythology, the books she devoured on history, and the treasures in Stanton Park itself which meant more to her than anything else in her life.

'I am very ignorant,' she thought now as she moved passed a bush covered with the white petals of the fragrant syringa.

Coming to Naples had been an education in itself, and yet in some ways it had been very frightening.

Cordelia reached the arbour where she and Mark Stanton had sat the night he had arrived and where he had spoken to her of love.

She had thought so often of his words and they seemed to repeat and re-repeat themselves in her mind, while she told herself she had never envisaged for one moment that he would say such things to her.

She had known that he was a man of action and a man born to command, so that it had been impossible for her to imagine that he would look into her heart and understand her secret dreams.

Now, since he had put it so clearly, she understood what she wanted of life – it was love!

She had not had a chance to speak intimately with him again. Always they had been surrounded by chattering socialites, or when he had called in the afternoon Lady Hamilton had been with them or David.

Sometimes Cordelia had glanced at him shyly, thinking she must have imagined that conversation under the starlit sky.

Yet she knew that he had swept away her fears and made things which had seemed so tangled and complicated quite simple.

Now she no longer thought of entering a Convent.

Instead she was sure – because Mark had said so – that one day she would find a man whom she would love and who would love her in return.

But of one thing she was quite sure. She would never find the sort of man she was seeking amongst the glittering, affected aristocrats of Naples.

Mark Stanton must have spoken very effectively to the Duca, for she had not seen him again and he no longer sent her flowers or effusive notes which made her heart beat apprehensively as soon as she saw his bold hand-writing.

These past days had therefore been quiet for her emotionally if not physically.

In fact there had seemed to be an endless stream of

parties, Receptions and visits to the Palace. She also helped to entertain the people who flocked to the British Embassy as if they needed reassurance.

Cordelia was aware of the Queen's incessant anxiety about the situation because the strain of it was beginning to react on Lady Hamilton.

It was not surprising that Her Majesty was perturbed when it was calculated that there were ten thousand French in Lombardy, twenty thousand along the coast around Genoa, and reports of the numbers of war-ships being fitted out in the Toulon dock-yards grew in size every day.

"The Queen believes herself to be threatened by land and sea with no help save for the British Navy," Lady Hamilton said to Cordelia.

She gave a deep sigh.

"The only person who can save us now is Sir Horatio Nelson!"

There was a softness in Lady Hamilton's voice when she spoke of the Naval hero and indeed she talked of him incessantly.

There was no doubt that he had made a tremendous impression when he had visited Naples as Captain of *The Agamemnon*.

He had been wounded with grape shot in a landing at Santa Cruz and with his arm having been sawn off by the ship's surgeon, he had sailed home to join the captains on half-pay at Bath.

With only one eye and one arm, his vivid personality made him so popular that he was the man to whom the country turned when news came of the huge armament being built by Napoleon in the Mediterranean.

Sir Horatio had set sail with fourteen first rate line-of-battleships but he had been hampered, as Mark Stanton knew, by losing sight of his frigates in a storm, by the shortness of stores, and by the damage to his ships.

Sir Horatio had written to Sir William Hamilton that if he had to move his fleet he would need provisions, frigates and good pilots.

"Sir William is distracted," Lady Hamilton explained.

She talked frankly to Cordelia and David as if she must confide her innermost thoughts to someone and perhaps relieve her own anxiety.

"Will Sir William be able to help Admiral Nelson?" David enquired.

"How can he?" Lady Hamilton replied. "The King has signed a document in which he vows never to victual or water British ships! As for providing him with frigates ...!"

Lady Hamilton threw up her arms and they knew that even the Queen would be afraid to favour the British with French Troops threatening them.

Now, sitting in the arbour overlooking the Bay, Cordelia deliberately put the thoughts of war, battleships, the French, and the menace of Napoleon, out of her mind.

To-day she wanted only to absorb the beauty of Naples and to forget everything else.

Butterflies were hovering over the camellias. The syringa blossom was beautiful and a white dove, one of many that flew wild in the Embassy Gardens, perched on the low stone balustrade in front of her and regarded her with inquisitive eyes.

She kept very still, while the soft 'coo' of the dove reminded her of the wood-pigeons in Stanton Park and she wondered if the house felt lonely now that there were only a few servants left in charge.

The shutters had been closed in all the principal rooms and there was no knowing when they would be opened again.

She had always imagined herself living at Stanton Park until David married, or perhaps until she herself left for another home.

In a way it had been heart-breaking, although she would not have admitted to her brother, to leave behind everything that was familiar, everything that was connected in her mind with her father and mother.

While her mother had adored David, her father to Cordelia was everything that she admired.

She had loved him blindly as a child might do, not dissecting or analysing her feelings, only knowing that she was happy when he was there.

Sir William reminded her a little of her father and she could understand how Lady Hamilton who, if the stories were to be believed, had lived an insecure and somewhat reprehensible life before she came to Naples, had found happiness with him.

He did not seem to mind the extravagantly amorous compliments or the obvious adoration that a great number of handsome Neapolitans felt for her.

'Perhaps marriage to a man who is so much older than one's self would be a mistake,' Cordelia thought.

Then she added that it might be very comforting to have a sense of protection and safety.

The idea of being married to a young man like the one who had pursued her in England, or to the Duca in Naples made her shudder.

The Duca particularly frightened her with his ardency which she sensed went much deeper than his words and by the expression in his eyes that she was too innocent to understand.

"I must not judge all men by the few I have met," Cordelia told herself with practical common sense.

She heard someone approaching along the path towards the arbour and thought it might be Mark Stanton.

If he had been told she was in the garden, she thought, he would guess she would go to the arbour to look at the view.

The footsteps came nearer, the evergreen branches of the syringa parted. Then with a sudden gasp of fear she saw it was not Mark Stanton as she expected but the Duca di Belina!

He came towards her with a smile on his lips, and she was unable to move, unable to do anything but stare at him with wide frightened eyes.

The Duco di Belina was understandably an exceedingly conceited man.

He had been the most important and eligible bachelor in Neapolitan Society since he was twenty years old.

At thirty he had sampled all the delights of the pleasure-loving Capital and found that women, from the highest to the lowest, were only too eager to offer him their favours.

In fact he could not remember when he had ever been repulsed or refused anything he demanded of a woman – until he met Cordelia.

Her beauty fascinated him from the first moment he set eyes on her.

He was satiated with the voluptuous charms that were offered him in Naples, in other parts of Italy and in every country bordering on the Mediterranean.

In contrast to dark, flashing eyes, a golden skin, and eager, hungry lips, Cordelia's small, classical features, her white skin and proud reserve excited him as he told himself he had never been excited before.

Determined that she should be his and knowing that with her social position he could offer nothing else but marriage, he proposed with the air of a King conferring a favour.

His astonishment when she refused him would to an outsider have been amusing.

But the Duca only assuaged the insult to his pride by explaining to himself that because Cordelia was English she would not be hurried and was therefore playing hard-to-get.

That Cordelia actively disliked him and was frightened of him, never entered his mind.

He was completely sure of his virile attractions where the female sex was concerned, since his long line of successes had given him an unshakable confidence that no woman was beyond his reach.

When Cordelia refused his suit he had gone to Lady Hamilton to enlist her help.

He found as he had expected that she was only too willing to assist him. Indeed she thought it an excellent idea to have another Englishwoman in such a position of importance in Naples.

Yet however skilfully Lady Hamilton pleaded the Duca's suit she made no impression on Cordelia.

To his astonishment the Duca found that the young English girl, far from being flattered by his attentions, was deliberately avoiding him and slipping out of his way in a manner he found more and more frustrating.

Where he had been attracted and undoubtedly enamoured by Cordelia's beauty, he was now driven almost to madness because she was so elusive.

His hunting instinct was aroused and he was determined, as he had never been determined in any project before, that she should marry him.

"No-one," he told himself, "and certainly not an unimportant Sea Captain, will prevent me from making her my wife!"

Concerned only with his own feelings and not understanding other people's he had been jolted out of his complacency when unexpectedly he had learnt the previous night in the Royal Palace that Cordelia's departure to Malta was imminent.

He tried to speak to her at the party to which she had accompanied Sir William and Lady Hamilton, but with an astuteness he had not expected Cordelia left the Royal Palace without the Duca getting her alone even for a few seconds.

He had therefore risen unprecedentedly early the following morning and decided he would call at the Palazzo Sessa before what would normally be considered a reasonable time.

He had the idea that Lady Hamilton would still be in bed and neither Cordelia's brother, nor her cousin, Mark Stanton, would be playing watch-dog at such an hour.

He knew he was right in his assumptions on being told by the servants that Cordelia was in the garden.

"I will announce myself!" he said firmly.

When the Major Domo would have protested he said a few sharp words in his own language which made the lackey bow respectfully and let him pass.

The Duca knew the garden at the Palazzo Sessa well.

He had philandered in almost every part of it with one attractive woman or another at the innumerable Receptions and Balls given by the British Ambassador.

In fact, he told himself with an amused smile as he walked

along the narrow paths, there was hardly a nook or a corner where he had not kissed a willing pair of lips or held a soft body quivering with passion in his arms.

When he pushed aside the syringa boughs and saw Cordelia sitting in the arbour, her fair hair haloed with sunshine, he thought she was even more beautiful and more desirable than he remembered.

He walked towards her, swaggering a little because he was well aware that he was a prepossessing figure of a man and exceedingly handsome.

"I thought I should find you here," he said in a voice that always seemed to inject into everything he said a kind of amorous undertone.

"I . . . I must . . . go back to the . . . house."

Cordelia would have risen to her feet but the Duca put his hand on her arm to prevent her from doing so and sat down beside her.

"I want to talk to you, Cordelia."

She thought it an impertinence that he should call her by her Christian name, but for the moment she was concerned only with the feeling of disgust which swept over her at the touch of his hand.

She was well aware also that her heart was beating frantically and her lips felt dry.

She could not understand why he frightened her so tremendously, she only knew that she longed to run away.

But to reach the path from the arbour she had to pass him and she knew he would not let her go.

"We have . . . nothing to . . . discuss," she managed to say with a tremendous effort.

"On the contrary there are many things," he said. "Is it really true that you are leaving to-morrow?"

"Yes . . . we are going to . . . Malta."

"Then that is something I must prevent you from doing."

"I . . . I am . . . going with my . . . brother and my . . . cousin, Captain Mark Stanton."

She had meant the words to sound firm and perhaps defiant, but instead there was a quiver in her voice and she knew it was because the Duca still had his hand on her bare arm.

She tried to move but realised that was a mistake because his fingers tightened.

"I love you, Cordelia!" he said. "You cannot sail away when you know I wish you to be my wife!"

"I have already . . . told Your Grace that while I am deeply . . . honoured by such a . . . suggestion, I cannot . . . marry you."

"Why not?"

"B.because . . . I do not . . . love you!"

He gave a little laugh that seemed to contain a threat in its very sound.

"I will teach you to love me, *Carissima*. I will teach you all about love. You will learn to want me as I want you!"

It seemed to Cordelia as if he drew nearer as he spoke and there was a fire behind his words which made her feel as if it leapt out from him to scorch her.

"No! No! I can never . . . love you! Never!"

"How can you be sure of that?" he asked. "You are so beautiful — so desirable! There is something about you which drives me crazy! I cannot sleep at night for thinking about you and I want you — God knows I want you — as I have never wanted a woman before!"

Now there was a raw note in the words which made Cordelia jump to her feet.

"Let me go!" she said. "I have told you that I can . . . never be your . . . wife!"

"And I am determined that you shall be!"

The Duca rose too and was now facing her, making it impossible for her to squeeze past him and escape.

With an effort she fought to control the panic she felt sweeping over her and to face him defiantly with her chin held high even though her lips trembled.

"Let me go! I have . . . nothing to say to you . . . nothing except that I will never . . . marry you and I am . . . leaving to-morrow!"

When she finished speaking her voice was hardly above a whisper. Yet as she saw the blaze in his eyes she knew that her very resistance had inflamed him to the point where he lost his self-control.

His arms went out towards her and as she fought against his strength feverishly, frantically, she screamed and screamed again . . .

*　　　*　　　*

Mark Stanton had also been saying good-bye . . .

He had only just announced to the Hamiltons the time that his ship would be ready to leave when he received a note from Gianetta asking him to dine with her.

"*I have something of the greatest importance to impart to you,*" the Princess wrote after her sprawling signature.

He was in fact intrigued by the postscript, and anyway he knew, after all they had meant to each other over the years it would be impossible for him to leave Naples without seeing her.

He discovered at the Palazzo Sessa that Cordelia would be well looked after that evening.

It had been arranged for them to attend a performance at the Theatre, at which the King and Queen were to be present, and then go on to a supper-party at the Palace.

"We shall be delighted if you would come with us, should you wish to do so," Lady Hamilton suggested.

Mark Stanton had however excused himself.

A Royal evening was something he found incredibly boring, and if he was honest with himself, he was prepared to admit he disliked the King.

He also found the Queen irritating despite the fact that he hoped there was a chance, because of her hatred for the French, that she might prove a good ally to Britain.

But the toadying Court Officials, the disloyal Italian Princelings who had scattered like a pack of cards before the French, disgusted him.

He had learnt that the tricolour flew high above the ramparts of many of the ancient patrician castles and their owners were, in school-boy parlance, 'sucking up' to those they expected would conquer them in a very short space of time.

It was therefore with a genuine sense of pleasure that Mark Stanton accepted the Princess's invitation and arrived at her Palazzo to find, as he had foreseen, that he was the only guest.

It was fortunate that the weather in mid-May was so warm that she could afford to wear the minimum amount of clothing.

Certainly the diaphanous gown she wore of gauze threaded with gold revealed rather than concealed her nakedness.

She, however, wore round her neck a magnificent necklace of emeralds, diamonds and rubies which with her swinging ear-rings gave her an almost oriental appearance.

Her dark eyes slanted at him invitingly and there was no need for her red lips to tell him how pleased she was to see him.

"Mark! Mark! How can you have neglected me so cruelly these past few days?"

"I have been concerned with repairing my ship," he replied automatically.

"And dancing attendance in the British Embassy," she added. "Is it the full-blown rose or the bud which attracts you?"

Mark Stanton did not answer but moved through the open windows of the magnificent Salon onto the balcony outside.

"I will not tease you," she said in a low voice, holding onto his arm. "I am only so glad you are here. All I want is to feel you near me and to tell you of my love."

He smiled at her quizzically and there was a mocking note in his voice as he said:

"I am honoured to receive such protestations, Gianetta."

"I love you, Mark, I never realised how much until the other night. And now, because of you, I have taken a very revolutionary decision."

"What is that?" he enquired.

He was slightly surprised by the serious way she spoke.

"I have decided to leave Naples."

"This is very unexpected."

"Because you will not marry me," she said, "you have

made all the men that I know here seem bores and nincom-poops!"

"I regret I should have had that effect," Mark Stanton said, but his eyes were twinkling.

"It is true!" the Princess said passionately. "Because you are the perfect lover, a man who makes all other men seem small and insignificant by comparison, I cannot stay here."

"In fact you seek 'pastures new'," he quoted.

She nodded her dark head so that her jewelled ear-rings jangled against the round column of her neck.

"I think I shall go to Paris!"

She knew it was a provocative statement and she looked at him under her eye-lashes to see his reaction.

"A good idea! When Napoleon gets tired of war he will set himself up a Court of some sort or other. You will un-doubtedly shine even in that city of beautiful women."

"That is what I thought," the Princess said with a little sigh. "But it has been a big decision to make, and by refusing me you have altered my whole life!"

"So I shall be responsible for whatever happens," Mark Stanton said.

He did not sound very perturbed and he raised the glass of champagne that the servant had brought to him to his lips.

"Yes, it will be your fault," the Princess said, "and al-though I shall seek someone like you in Paris, in Vienna, perhaps even in Moscow, I know I shall never find another Man of the Sea to capture my heart as you have done."

They dined by candlelight in her Boudoir.

It was impossible for Mark Stanton not to be moved by the love, if that was the right word for it, that he saw in the Princess's eyes or the hunger in her lips.

When dinner was over and the servants left the room Mark leant back in his chair with a glass of brandy in his hand and asked:

"What was the important secret you have to tell me?"

The Princess glanced over her shoulder to make certain they were alone and lowered her voice.

"I dined at the French Ministry last night."

He raised his eye-brows, but he did not speak.

"It was a small party," the Princess went on, "and the Minister spoke freely."

"You mean he believed he knew where your sympathies lie?"

The Princess's eyes flickered.

"I have been . . . useful to him on . . . several occasions."

Mark Stanton sipped his brandy.

"The Minister told us what Napoleon Bonaparte's aims are in the Mediterranean."

Mark was still, his eyes watched the Princess.

"He means to take Egypt!"

It was what he had suspected, but it was a blow to hear it confirmed.

"His plan," the Princess continued, "is eventually to conquer India."

Mark Stanton drew in his breath. It was audacious and wildly ambitious but to the young Corsican who had achieved so much already it was possible.

"French agents," the Princess almost whispered, "are endeavouring to raise a revolt against the British in Hindustan."

"How many men has Bonaparte in Toulon?"

There was a pause before the Princess replied:

"They say about eighty thousand!"

Mark Stanton was appalled, but it did not show in his expression.

"Thank you," he said quietly.

"Is that – all you have to say?"

"I could express myself more eloquently if we were closer."

"That is what I want!"

She rose from the table.

They moved into the Bedroom next door. Discreetly lit, the shadows were full of mystery, her special fragrance scented the air.

She turned to face him, and he removed first her long ear-rings, then the necklace of rubies and emeralds.

Then he pulled her roughly into his arms and his mouth crushed hers.

The fire which had always existed between them burst into flame.

The passion of it scorched and consumed them both with a wild, irresistible blaze, rising and falling as the hours passed until the night faded and the dawn came up pale and golden over the misty sea.

They slept from sheer exhaustion ...

When Mark Stanton awoke it was to find that it was far later than he had expected and he had broken his rule of returning to his lodgings before the world was awake.

He lay for a moment against the silken pillows and looked at Gianetta asleep beside him.

She was very beautiful in repose and her dark hair fell over her bare shoulders and her eye-lashes swept her cheeks.

He wondered as he regarded her why he found it impossible to give her the love she wanted from him.

She roused him passionately and there was also, because she was intelligent, a mutual interest that did not entirely rely on physical attraction.

But he knew that what she offered was not enough.

Passion would fade in time and he knew that he demanded a great deal more than passion in the woman he would make his wife.

He wanted, he told himself with a cynical twist to his lips, a love such as he had described to Cordelia.

He had often wondered since that night when they had sat together in the arbour how he had been able to speak to her as he had, to explain love in terms which he had never before consciously used to himself.

And yet the explanation of what she was feeling and what she feared had come to him almost clairvoyantly so that he had known even as he spoke that he was saying the right thing, and that he could help her.

Everything which he had told her had been dormant in him, though never had he consciously realised the truth of it.

Mark Stanton had always been a man of action.

When he was only twenty, one of his relatives had sent him to the West Indies in a Merchant ship.

It had given him an insight into a way of life which he had not known existed.

He had been appalled at the manner in which the crew were treated and the hardship endured by the Officers.

He was to learn that a ship at sea could be a hell and an inferno for those who sailed in her, and he was determined that when his time came to command he would treat his seamen as human beings, not animals.

The ambition that was born in him on his first voyage was eventually to command his own ship and, because he was driven by his enthusiasm and used his brain, he found himself in that position in a surprisingly few years.

His father was not rich like many of his relatives and Mark realised that he needed money.

In the Mediterranean there were prizes to be won.

The crew of a Christian ship took a percentage of every cargo they filched from the Infidel, and the Captain was paid a commission on the sale of every slave who was brought alive into Malta.

The Captain's share of the spoils of war and piracy were large and Mark was an extremely successful Commander.

He had no need to hawk his services.

His reputation kept him always in demand, and in fact the Grand Master, the Prince de Rohan, with whom he was friendly, had suggested that he might consider becoming a Knight of St. John.

Mark had laughed at him.

"I admire your Order, Your Eminence, I respect the fighting ability of your Knights, but the vow of chastity would sound a mockery on my lips!"

The Grand Master had sighed.

"It is our loss, Captain Stanton. I would have liked above all things to ask you to be an Instructor in my new School of Mathematics and Naval Sciences."

"I am always ready to be of assistance, Your Eminence. You have only to ask me," Mark Stanton replied, and he found himself executing commissions for the Order on many occasions.

But as he had said to the Grand Master, the vow of chastity was not for him.

After a long voyage the relaxation he found in the soft warmth of a woman was something he looked forward to and which he felt gave him strength to return to an arduous command.

There were women in ports all over the Mediterranean who waited and longed for his return.

But while he was pleased to see them and accepted their love, he knew when he sailed away that they in reality meant little or nothing in his life.

Perhaps Gianetta meant more than the others – he was not sure. He seldom thought of her unless he came to Naples.

Beautiful though she was, he told himself that he could never tie himself to her or to any other woman like her.

He rose gently from the bed.

When he was dressed he wondered for a moment if he should awaken her to say good-bye, then he decided it was better not to.

There was no point in an emotional scene, which could only be an anti-climax to the passion they had enjoyed during the night.

Going out onto the balcony Mark Stanton picked a red rose from the profusion of flowers growing over the balustrade.

He went back into the bed-room and laid it in front of Gianetta on the white sheet.

He knew she would understand its message. Then quietly he went from the room closing the door behind him.

He took the carriage that was plying for hire in the crowded streets back to his lodgings.

When he had bathed and changed he looked at the clock with an almost comical expression of dismay.

He was well aware that the Baron and David would think him very remiss not being at the dock-yard to supervise what remained to be done to the ship before they could sail in the morning.

He was quite certain that David would be already there, but just in case he had waited for him at the Embassy as he had done on previous mornings, Mark Stanton called at the Palazzo Sessa.

"Is His Lordship here?" he asked the Major Domo who greeted him effusively.

"No, Captain, His Lordship left early for the dock-yard."

It was what he had expected. Then just as he was about to tell the driver to move on he asked:

"And Lady Cordelia? Is she awake?"

"Her Ladyship is in the garden, Captain. She was up early and she went there alone, but she has just been joined by a gentleman."

"A gentleman?" Mark Stanton enquired.

"Yes, Captain, the Duca di Belina."

For a moment Mark Stanton felt he could not have heard the man aright.

Then he walked quickly up the steps of the Embassy and without waiting for the Major Domo to follow him passed out onto the terrace down the steps and into the garden.

He was almost certain that he would find Cordelia in the arbour where they had sat and talked of love.

With a perception that was unusual he thought that she would have gone there to say good-bye to Naples and have a last look at the light on the Bay.

He moved quickly along the twisting paths looking through the bushes on either side of him in case he should catch a glimpse of Cordelia.

Then before he reached the arbour he heard her scream.

*　　　*　　　*

The Duca had not expected such resistance from anyone so small and fragile as Cordelia.

But she fought him like a tigress, twisting and turning against his arms, beating at him with her fists and striking at him as he pulled her relentlessly closer and closer to him, his lips seeking hers.

She screamed and turned her head from side to side.

But he knew it was only a question of seconds before she would find it impossible to go on fighting and his superior strength must prevail.

Her breath was coming sobbingly from between her lips,

and just as he sensed that she could no longer go on fighting, he felt a hand catch him at the back of the collar.

It dragged him forcibly from Cordelia and a fist smashed into his face sending him staggering against the seat on which they had been sitting.

The Duca gave an exclamation of fury and saw Mark Stanton facing him, his blues eyes blazing like those of an avenging angel.

"How dare you strike me!" the Duca exclaimed, speaking in Italian.

He was however no coward and his achievements in the art of self-defence were legendary among his contemporaries.

He was considered the best swordsman in Naples, he was a crack-shot, and he kept himself exceedingly fit in a gymnasium he had had specially constructed in his Ducal Palace.

He did not particularly care for fighting with bare fists, but his temper was up and there was no time to suggest more civilised methods of conflict.

He rushed at Mark Stanton like an angry bull, expecting to floor him as easily as he had floored his opponents at the boxing-school he sometimes attended.

But Mark Stanton's body was as hard as iron and his fists carried a punch which the Duca was experienced enough to know would knock him cold if it landed on his chin.

Neither of the men paid any attention to Cordelia who moved out of their way by squeezing herself behind the wooden seat. It was at least a protection against their flying arms and quick-moving bodies.

She could hardly believe that Mark had come to her rescue at a moment when she realised she could no longer go on fighting.

She had known she must surrender from sheer weakness and that the Duca's lips would take possession of hers.

She had thought frantically in some part of her terrified mind that she would die at the touch of him.

Then just when she had lost a very unequal battle and

she could no longer breathe, she had miraculously found herself free.

The two men were fighting with a ferocity that made her tremble, and yet she could not take her eyes from them.

They each seemed to be impervious to the other's blows, but there was blood running down the Duca's chin from the corner of his mouth, while Mark's face was untouched.

He was the taller, but the Duca's body was heavier and there was something fanatical in the way he threw out his fists which made Cordelia afraid for her cousin.

Then suddenly it was over.

Mark caught the Duca an uppercut which lifted him off his feet.

He staggered backwards and losing his balance fell over the low parapet into an oleander bush.

There was the crash of broken branches. Then he was still, his feet stretched out in front of him almost ludicrously.

Wide-eyed and trembling Cordelia came from behind the wooden seat.

Mark was looking down at his broken knuckles; his coat was slightly disarranged and his cravat was ruffled, but otherwise he appeared to be quite unconcerned by what had occurred.

She moved towards him and he saw by the pallor of her face and the expression in her eyes how frightened she was.

He put his arm round her shoulders and found that she was trembling.

"It is all right, Cordelia."

As if she could not help herself she hid her face against his shoulder.

"He . . . frightened me," she whispered.

"I know," Mark Stanton said, "but he is unlikely to do so again."

He glanced towards the Duca who was lying completely immobile in the oleander bush.

"Let us go back to the house."

Cordelia was still trembling, but the matter-of-fact manner in which Mark spoke had its effect.

With an effort at self-control which he admired she moved away from him.

"I will . . . get some . . . lotions and . . . bandages . . . for your . . . hands."

Her breath came in little gasps between the words.

"That would be very kind," Mark answered. "Fortunately I heal quickly."

She moved ahead of him along the narrow path and he knew as he followed her that she was trying hard to walk with dignity and to hold her chin high.

They reached the terrace and Cordelia saw with relief that there was no-one there.

"I . . . I will . . . f.find what you . . . require," she said hesitatingly.

Mark Stanton after one look at her pale face drew her to one of the cushion-covered seats and made her sit down on it.

"I will send a servant, then we can see how good you are at bandaging," he said.

He smiled at her, vanished for a few moments, then returned to sit down beside her and take her hand in his.

"I am sorry this has happened, Cordelia."

She looked at him piteously, and he saw that her grey eyes were still stricken as if at some nameless horror.

"I would not have . . . believed that a . . . man would . . . behave like . . . that," she said hesitatingly after a moment.

"Not all men are like the Duca," Mark replied. "You must be sensible, Cordelia, and forget what has happened."

"You . . . said that he would not come . . . near me again," she murmured almost childishly.

"I thought I was dealing with a gentleman of honour," Mark Stanton replied. "You must forgive me, Cordelia, for not being a very experienced guardian. Another time I will trust no-one!"

"I could not . . . bear there to be . . . another time," she said. "Perhaps . . ."

He knew what he was going to say before she said it. The thought of the Convent had come back into her mind and he said quickly :

"No! That is not the answer. Besides, I would not expect you to play coward."

"Coward?"

He felt his accusation had jolted her.

"It is cowardly to run away from life," he said. "What you experienced a few moments ago, Cordelia was very unpleasant, but you are sensible enough to realise that there are always penalties attached to everything."

"Penalties?" she asked.

"Because men find you so beautiful they may tend to lose their heads and behave in an uncontrolled manner."

He saw the surprise in her expression and he went on:

"But we are dealing with a Neapolitan, and we will not be in Naples again for a very long time."

He smiled as he went on:

"You are going to an island where there is a large number of young men, but they have all taken the vow of chastity. That in itself should be a safeguard. At the same time, Cordelia, you are very beautiful!"

He saw the colour come into her cheeks at the compliment and she looked away from him shyly.

"D.do you ... really ... think so?"

"I think there is one thing about which we must agree," Mark Stanton replied, "and that is always to tell each other the truth. When I say that you are beautiful, Cordelia, I mean it!"

"Thank ... you."

A servant appeared with bandages, a cream with which to salve Mark's broken knuckles and a bowl.

Another servant brought wine and Mark insisted on Cordelia drinking a little.

"It is too ... early in the day," she protested.

"You have suffered a shock," he insisted. "If we were in England I would prescribe a warm, sweet drink, but you know as well as I do that in this place it would take hours to prepare!"

She laughed at that and sipped the wine obediently.

It brought the colour back into her cheeks and he saw that the stricken look had gone from her eyes.

He then allowed her to bandage the knuckles of both his hands.

"You are very expert!" he said.

"Mama insisted that I should learn how to look after people when they were sick or if they injured themselves. Papa used to laugh at the lessons she gave me, but I cannot help feeling that if we are in Malta and men are wounded I might be of some assistance."

"I doubt that," Mark Stanton replied. "The Knights have a most efficient Hospital. The novices take their turn in nursing the sick."

"That is something David will not like," Cordelia said with a smile. "He is always impatient of people who are ill. I suppose it is because he is so strong himself."

"David will have to serve his turn in the Hospital," Mark Stanton said dryly.

"He will want to do his duty," Cordelia replied, "but I wish I could do it for him."

Mark Stanton looked at his hands.

"I shall know where to come if I am in any trouble."

He rose to his feet.

"I am sure, Cordelia, you do not wish to be here when the Duca recovers consciousness. Will you go to your bed-room, or would you prefer to come with me to the dock-yard?"

She raised her eyes to his.

"I would not wish to be a . . . nuisance to you."

He looked down at her and there was no mockery in his smile as he said:

"You could never be that!"

Chapter Four

With the breeze behind them the sails of the *St. Jude* emblazoned with the Eight-Pointed Cross were carrying the ship smoothly over the blue sea.

Seated in a shady corner of the deck Cordelia was fascinated by the activity taking place around her.

Men were running like monkeys up the complicated rigging, there were frequent alterations to the sails and orders came peremptorily from the bridge where Mark Stanton was in charge.

She had not expected the *St. Jude* to be so large, seeing that it was privately owned, but she realised as soon as she came on board that it was in fact a Man-o'-War in every sense of the word.

She had listened to Mark explaining to David how the Order had revised its Naval policy at the beginning of the century.

"Instead of a striking force consisting only of galleys, which were oar-propelled vessels with auxiliary sails," he said, "these have been progressively reduced and instead round-bottomed sailing Ships were introduced."

"And they have proved effective?" David asked.

"The same type of battleship has been built by every country in Europe, and of course by the Barbary Pirates," he answered.

David had looked at the cannons and said a little doubtfully :

"Surely those are not large enough for some of the new vessels built by the French?"

"That is true," Mark Stanton admitted, "but they prove very effective against the majority of ships we encounter."

He looked at the sailors hurrying about the deck and went on :

"The Maltese cannoneers are the best in the world and there is no doubt that it is due to their skill that the vessels of the Order owe their success in combat."

"I should like to see them firing these cannons," David said with shining eyes.

"You will see a fight soon enough," Mark Stanton replied, "and you will find it is very rare if on the second run in the masts of the enemy are not brought down."

All the rest of the afternoon David talked to Ludwig von Wütenstein of battles. Especially of Jacques de Chambrai, a skilled sailor of the Order who fired 328 salvos of cannon in two and a half hours!

"In one year," David cried gleefully, "he took six Barbary Corsairs and eight hundred slaves."

Cordelia was not surprised when after they had been at sea for only a day David was talking enthusiastically of the ship he planned to own himself.

Now he came running along the deck to throw himself down beside her and say with an air of excitement that she always found irresistible:

"I must have a ship of my own, Cordelia, and I have no wish to wait for several years as Mark is suggesting I should."

"I expect he is talking good sense," Cordelia replied. "It would be wise to do your four 'caravans' before you become an owner."

"If you think I am going to wait until I am twenty-four," David exclaimed, "you are very mistaken! When I come of age in October I will be in control of my fortune and I can then give instructions to the ship-yard."

Cordelia was silent.

She was well aware that a ship would cost a great deal to build.

While it was accepted that David's personal fortune should become the property of the Order on his death, she knew that their relatives and Trustees were hoping that on attaining his majority he would spend carefully.

They had heard that many of the Knights were wildly extravagant.

"Of course I realise," David was saying, "that I cannot touch any of my inheritance that is entailed for the benefit of the Estate, but at the same time my own fortune will be in my hands on the 12th of October, and after that no-one need try to dissuade me from doing what I wish to do."

He spoke truculently and Cordelia said gently:

"Any opposition you may have encountered, David, has only arisen because our relatives love you and wish perhaps to safe-guard you against yourself."

"I have no wish to be safe-guarded," David retorted. "Ludwig tells me the Order are very grateful for privately owned vessels because their own Navy is not as large as it was and is insignificant compared to that of the British or the French."

Cordelia gave a little sigh.

She was quite certain that, head-strong as usual, David would do as he wished and she thought perhaps the only person who could make him see sense was Mark Stanton.

Ever since they had come on board and David had seen his cousin in a position of authority, his attitude showed a respect which had not been there previously.

"In fact," Cordelia told herself with a little smile, "I am certain that by the time we reach Malta, David will be hero-worshipping Mark."

She had been so intent on listening to her brother that she had not noticed that having left the bridge, Mark was approaching them.

She was aware of his presence without turning round. Then she felt his hand on her shoulder.

"You are all right?" he asked, "and quite comfortable?"

"It is wonderful being at sea," she replied, "and travelling in such a magnificent ship."

She saw the pleasure in his eyes.

He sat down beside her as David jumped to his feet and hurried to look at something which had attracted his attention.

When he was out of ear-shot Cordelia said in a low voice:

"As I think you must have realised, David is determined to buy a Ship of his own."

"There is no reason why he should not do so when he can afford it," Mark Stanton replied.

"That will be in October when he comes of age," Cordelia said. "I am sure you think it would be better to wait a while."

He looked at her with a little smile.

"You sound like a mother hen fussing over her obstreperous chick," he teased. "Do not concern yourself unduly. I will look after David and not allow him to make too many expensive mistakes during his first year in Malta."

Cordelia gave a little sigh of relief.

"Thank you," she said. "You are so kind. I cannot imagine what we would have done without you."

She spoke without thinking.

Then she remembered how he had saved her from the Duca and the colour rose in her cheeks.

His uncanny perception where she was concerned made him know what she was thinking, and he said gently:

"Forget it. It is all over. One should never look back, but always forward."

"Is that your philosophy?" she asked curiously.

"There is always so much to do ahead of us," he answered. "It seems to me an incredible waste of time to regret the past when we can do nothing about it."

"How wise and sensible you are!"

"Unfortunately wisdom comes only with age. When I was young I was like David. I acted first and thought afterwards!"

Cordelia laughed.

"You speak as if you were already grey-headed!"

"One grows old quickly when one is at sea," he answered.

As if what he was saying alerted him to the responsibility of his command, he rose to his feet and walked back to the bridge shouting at the look-out in the crow's-nest at the top of the mast to keep good watch.

Cordelia realised that the ship's crew must always be alert: this was essential for their own protection.

To be taken by surprise was to lose everything they valued, including their lives.

But there were no incidents on the voyage to Malta, and when at last they had their first sight of the island bathed in sunshine, it seemed to be the Golden Paradise which David had yearned to reach.

Cordelia knew from her maps that the archipelago was small. In fact Malta, Mark had told her, was but seventeen miles long and nine miles broad.

He had made David work out the longitude and the latitude of the group of islands which lay at the cross-roads of the Mediterranean, half way between Gibraltar and Egypt.

But it was not its strategical position that was exciting as the *St. Jude* drew nearer, but the mile upon mile of fortified curtain and bastion rising out of the sea itself.

It gave an impression of strength and impregnability which was indescribable.

The powerful shapes of the massive forts dominated the craggy outline of the coast and when they were nearer still Cordelia could see that the high surfaces of the Valetta fortifications seemed to form a plinth for the lace-like intricacies of Baroque Palaces and Churches.

"Malta! Malta at last!" David cried at her side.

There was a note of exaltation in his voice and his eyes held the expression of a Visionary.

"Do not expect too much, dearest," Cordelia begged. "I could not bear you to be disappointed."

"It will not only be what I see and hear in Malta which matters," David replied, "but what I feel in my soul."

Cordelia slipped her arm through his.

"Your dream will come true because you believe."

"Yes, I believe!" David repeated and she felt it was in the nature of a vow.

Cordelia was to discover that Malta was an island of contrasts.

Although the impressive Auberges and Palace commanded her admiration, she found Valetta's narrow streets teeming with life were so fascinating that she wanted to spend hours just looking at them.

When they docked Mark Stanton insisted on taking her immediately to the house where she would be staying and introducing her to her host and hostess with whom he was already acquainted.

Count Manduca was Maltese and his ancestors had lived in Malta long before the Knights had been granted sovereignty by Charles V, Emperor of the Holy Roman Empire.

The Count was married to an Englishwoman, and their sons, who had been brought up in Malta now lived abroad.

"We are delighted to welcome you, Lady Cordelia," the Count said with an old world grace that made Cordelia think of William Hamilton.

"It is for me a pleasure I cannot express to entertain one of my country-women," the Countess told her. "I am only afraid I shall bore you with all my questions about England, which I have not visited for twenty years."

"I shall be only too happy to tell you anything you wish to know," Cordelia replied, "if you will answer my questions about Malta!"

The Countess laughed and showed Cordelia around her beautifully furnished house which stood in one of the main streets of Valetta.

"We have also a Villa in the country," she said, "where we will stay later in the summer when it becomes too hot in the City."

Cordelia said good-bye to David and Mark, and she knew she would not see them again until the following day.

But because she was so eager to explore Valetta she was up early in the morning and the Countess showed her the outside of some of the famous Auberges with their magnificent stone carvings and the shops which were unlike any she had seen before.

The goods that were brought to Malta as a great trading Port, either legitimately or because they had been captured on the high seas, made the City a melting-pot of East and West which was unique.

There were goldsmiths and silversmiths, vendors of rich Eastern brocades, curios and precious stones.

There were makers of carved and inlaid furniture, bird-fanciers and cobblers.

What fascinated Cordelia most were the stands on which

sweets, spices and rare tropical fruits were displayed, but there were other stalls with glittering rapiers, enamelled poniards and gold-hilted swords.

"I never imagined anything could be so fascinating!" she told the Countess.

Her hostess smiled.

"These people pander to the luxurious tastes of four hundred noble warriors," she replied, "and many of the Knights are very wealthy."

It seemed somehow incongruous to Cordelia when she remembered that all the Knights took the vow of poverty. But she remembered their possessions only passed to the Order when they died, and many were not prepared to deny themselves every comfort during their lifetime.

Meanwhile she contented herself with trying to take in all the beauty, the colour and the unusualness of Valetta.

She knew of course that David had first to be a *Novice* and that he would not take part in the solemn ceremony of Investiture for some months.

Then he would become a Knight of St. John which was the final profession of his faith. It could be dissolved only by death, dispensation or disgrace.

The afternoon after they had arrived David came to see her, thrilled with everything he had seen and the welcome he had received in his Tongue.

Cordelia felt she had already lost him as a brother; that she now only belonged to his past and could take no part in his future.

The Anglo-Bavarian Tongue which had only been opened for six years overlooked the Marsamuscette harbour and was a fine building which had been the Palace of the Bailiff of Acre.

David was very impressed by its magnificence, and he also informed Cordelia that the Knights of his Tongue had a special Military Post, a Chapel, a play-ground and a Gallery.

"We are trained in the discipline of arms on the ramparts," David enthused, "and we have to attend military practice and shooting at least three times a week."

"You will enjoy that," Cordelia smiled.

"It is very important that we should be proficient in the art of war," David said seriously. "Everyone here seems to talk of nothing else."

"Oh, David, I hope not!" Cordelia said impulsively.

"I only hope hostilities do not start before I have a chance to learn everything the instructors can teach me."

He chattered away and was so excited that Cordelia did not like to dampen his enthusiasm with her own apprehensions.

He had brought with him a servant whom Mark had recommended to him, and he wanted Cordelia to meet the man.

Giuseppe Vella was small, dark-skinned, aged about thirty. Cordelia liked his honest eyes and respectful attitude. She was sure David could trust him.

She was also certain that no one could be a more reliable judge of a man's character than Mark.

"Vella can inform me of many things I want to know," David said.

"I am sure that will be a great help," Cordelia smiled and said to the Maltese, "I am so glad that you will look after my brother."

Vella bowed.

"I will serve my Master faithfully and to the best of my ability."

When David had gone and Mark Stanton called, Cordelia thanked him for finding David a servant and she asked if it was true that Malta was anticipating enemy action.

Mark Stanton hesitated before he replied, for he did not wish to admit to Cordelia of all people that he was extremely perturbed by the situation in Valetta.

When he had last been in Malta he had been well aware that there were French spies moving about the defences and doubtless sending reports if not actual plans to Bonaparte.

It must have been impossible for the Grand Master not to realise the dangers of Malta's position.

It was almost incredible that von Hompesch should have done nothing about it.

Mark Stanton had expected to find a great deal of activity

taking place, but to his astonishment von Hompesch had made no attempt to remedy any deficiencies or to strengthen the fortifications.

The previous March Mark Stanton had been in Malta when the French Admiral de Brueys requested some repairs to one of his battleships while his fleet waited off-shore.

Uncertain of the intentions of the French, von Hompesch had ordered a general Alert.

Everyone in Malta had noticed that the muster of men amounted to little more than a third of what was considered necessary to defend the island.

But Admiral de Brueys however had set about allaying the fears of the garrison, making himself particularly pleasant to the Grand Master.

It was beautiful Spring weather and curious watchers from the roof-tops of the old capital of Notabile could see and admire a flotilla of seventeen warships anchored a mile out to sea.

That was three months ago and Mark Stanton had felt certain that while he had been away von Hompesch would have trained more artillery men.

When this morning he had asked for an audience with the Grand Master he found that he had in fact spent the three months since the French Admiral's visit reviving old ceremonies and religious festivals which had long been abandoned as being out of date.

Speaking quietly, without allowing any sign of his surprise or dis-satisfaction at the Grand Master's behaviour to show in his voice or in his bearing, Mark Stanton had told him the secret information that had been imparted to him by the Princess.

"Can you really credit that Napoleon Bonaparte would attempt to acquire Egypt?" von Hompesch asked almost contemptuously.

"I cannot conceive for what other reason he is building so large a Fleet in the Mediterranean, Your Eminence," Mark Stanton replied. "If he needed ships to defend the northern coastline of France against the British, he would have used the ship-yards of Boulogne or Le Havre."

"I see your point," the Grand Master conceded.

"On his way to Egypt," Mark Stanton went on, "Bonaparte will pass directly by Malta. It is obvious that he will wish to water and perhaps to re-victual his ships."

"You know the regulations of 1756 as well as I do, Captain Stanton," the Grand Master replied. "Only four ships can enter the Grand Harbour at one time."

"And you are able to enforce such a regulation, Your Eminence?"

"There is no reason to believe that any force will be necessary," the Grand Master said coldly. "We have the support of Russia and Austria, neither of whom would allow Malta to be attacked."

"I hope you are right, Your Eminence."

Mark Stanton bowed formally, thanked the Grand Master for granting him an audience and left the Palace.

He wended his way through the magnificent rooms with their Gobelin tapestries and frieze of frescoes illustrating the Grand Siege of 1565, and thought bitterly that he would have been treated in a very different manner if de Rohan had been alive.

The Prince had been a Grand Master that Mark Stanton could really admire.

He used to smile at his own family motto, which translated read: "I can't be King; I won't be Duke; I am Rohan!"

He was so progressive, so broad-minded. He kept the latest scientific and economic works beside his bed and rose at day-break to read them.

He was accessible and affable to everyone, but he would never have faced the position as it was at the moment with the limp, apathetic optimism of von Hompesch.

"He is living in cloud-cuckoo land," Mark said to himself.

But there was no point in explaining all this to Cordelia. It would only worry her and he wanted her to enjoy Malta.

He had not yet decided what should be done when she was ready to leave, but he had already told himself that his young cousin was his responsibility and it would be up to him to find some way of getting her safely back to England.

The Countess Manduca not only wished to show Cordelia

the architectural beauties of Malta, she also wished to entertain her socially.

That Cordelia was staying with a Maltese family was due to an arrangement made by the Grand Master de Rohan before his death.

It was quite usual for relatives to accompany prospective Knights to Malta, and as David had no father or mother he had decided that Cordelia should be his companion.

De Rohan had for some years tried to bridge the gulf that existed between the Maltese nobility and the Knights.

In every office of the island, except that of the Bishop and the Grand Prior who were sometimes Maltese, the lowest Knight was of more importance than the highest Maltese.

De Rohan held soirées to which Maltese ladies were invited, and he encouraged them to patronise the theatre of which he was an enthusiast.

He even created new titles and held all-night Balls.

He knew it would please the Maltese community if the sister of an Earl and a member of one of the noblest families in England stayed with the Count and Countess Manduca.

It was however Mark Stanton who arranged that Cordelia should be shown the Auberges by one of the Conventional Chaplains – a Priest of the Order – who knew more about the treasures collected over the centuries than anyone else.

She was entranced by the Council Chamber lined with magenta and canary brocade, with the walls and ceilings of the Auberge de Provence painted with green, crimson, beige and blue arabesques and flowers.

The cut-glass chandeliers from Murano, rugs from Damascus, carved sideboards from Amsterdam, china from Dresden, and closets from Lisbon had all been presents to the Order.

She also admired the huge stone staircases with heavy Baroque carvings and garlandings, and the enclosed courts where there were fountains and orange trees.

In every Auberge, she learnt, the Knights ate their meals off solid silver dishes.

"Have you known my cousin, Captain Stanton, for long,

Father?" she asked the Chaplain as they walked from one to another.

"For several years, Lady Cordelia," he replied. "He has a high standard of seamanship which is an example to all our young Knights."

Cordelia looked surprised and the Chaplain continued:

"Captain Stanton's consideration for his crew and his magnaminity to those he captures on the high seas shows Christianity at its best."

She was touched by the Chaplain's voice and the sincerity in his words.

Yet she had thought that Mark was hard, cynical and ruthless!

"That was before I knew him," she told herself and remembered his kindness when she had been frightened.

One of the most interesting places Cordelia was taken to see by the Chaplain was the Hospital or Sacred Infirmary.

"The Hospitals," he explained, "as I expect you know, Lady Cordelia, are the *raison d'être* of the Order. They are essentially the most sacred service of a true Knight."

He paused to say impressively:

"Even our enemies respect our Hospitals."

"I have read," Cordelia said, "that when the Christians were driven from Jerusalem, the Moslems allowed the Hospitallers to keep their Infirmary until the sick were healed."

"That is true," the Chaplain answered, "and the first act of the Knights on reaching Cyprus, then Rhodes, and lastly Malta was to improvise a Hospital."

There was however certainly nothing which justified the word 'improvised' about the Hospital in Valetta.

It stood on the shore of the Grand Harbour and the Great Ward measured 185 feet in length.

The Chaplain explained that the Hospital provided for the sick and wounded of all races, creeds and colour free of charge. Slaves were also admitted.

"In the past," the Chaplain told Cordelia, "every Knight would work in the Hospital and each Tongue had its day of duty."

"But not now?" Cordelia queried.

"Only the novices now nurse the sick, and sadly the Grand Masters who waited upon the poorest patient once a week only visit here occasionally."

Cordelia learnt that many changes had been made in the last ten years including the closing of wards and private rooms.

The silver plate which had astonished visitors in the seventeenth century as it was used by every patient was now kept for the affluent.

Yet there were still 370 beds with canopies and 365 without for fever patients.

There was also a Women's Hospital with 250 beds which took in foundlings and bastards. These were boarded out to foster-mothers at the expense of the Order.

The Chaplain then took Cordelia to the Church of St. John which was the pride of the Order.

Dedicated to St. John the Baptist, its most revered relic was a portion of the Saint's arm.

Centuries had transformed the original severe and monastic building into a mausoleum for the finest and best of European chivalry.

Cordelia looked at the swords and helmets of ancient warriors, at the Grand Cross of Jean de la Valette and the ikon of the Madonna attributed to St. Luke.

It seemed to her that the Knights whose bones lay beneath the floor, each covered by a tablet with their heraldic arms in inlaid mosaic, had imbued with their courage and idealism the very air.

She could feel them near her, men who had dedicated their lives to the service of God and had died as they lived with a prayer on their lips.

Theirs was the great ideal which had existed for seven centuries surmounting even defeat and expulsion.

"For Christ and St. John!"

She could hear the cry echoing down the years, inspiring the young and ardent, defending the weak, healing the sick!

"Please God, take care of David," she prayed. "Keep him true to his beliefs and his dream. Let him never fail himself!"

Raising her head she looked at the exquisite beauty of the glass windows and at the statues of the Saints, and felt almost as if she was receiving a special blessing.

Religion had always played a big part in Cordelia's life.

Her mother had been very religious and she had been instructed in the Catholic faith from the time she was a small child.

She accepted it as a part of her life even as she accepted that she breathed, ate and slept, and it was so familiar that she knew it had inspired her in the same way as it had David.

And now, because she was grateful, she thanked God and her prayer had a reality about it that she had not felt on other occasions.

She was about to rise from her knees when she thought of something else.

"Let me find love," she prayed, "the love that Mark told me about . . . the love that will not frighten me . . . but which is pure and divine."

She felt in that moment of prayer as if something within herself reached out towards what she sought.

She could not explain it in words, she felt it must be an awakening perhaps of her heart or of her spirit, and that because of what she felt she was growing in stature.

"When I am in love," Cordelia told herself, "I shall cease to be a child and I shall become a woman."

It was an intriguing idea and as she rose from her knees there was a smile on her lips which made her look more beautiful than she had ever looked before.

*   *   *

Cordelia hoped she would see Mark during the afternoon, but he sent a message to say that he was dining at the Grand Master's Palace and David, she knew, was dining in his own Auberge.

She felt a little neglected. At the same time she knew she had to be sensible and that from now on she must learn to be more independent.

However to be alone at home was very different from being alone in a strange country, staying in a strange house with strangers.

The Count and Countess could not have been kinder, but their interests were different to hers, their friends were just names of people she had never met, and when they did not talk of the Knights it was hard to keep the conversation going.

Cordelia began to wonder how long she should stay in Malta.

She had to face the fact that her presence would mean very little to David and it was doubtful if she would see much of him.

She was quite sure that as soon as it was possible he would beg to be sent on a 'caravan' and she knew that when he was away she would find every day her anxiety and fears for his safety would increase.

She found herself almost resenting, although she knew it was ridiculous, the fact that she was now of so little importance to her brother that it was unlikely it would matter to him whether she stayed or whether she left Malta.

She saw now only too clearly how from his point of view it would have been so much better if she could have been married before he started his training as a Knight.

And before he dedicated his whole life, as he wished to do, to the Order of St. John.

But when she thought of the two men who had offered for her, she knew that any unhappiness she might suffer alone would be better than being tied to a husband she disliked.

Especially one like the Duca, who both frightened and disgusted her.

She thought she could never be sufficiently grateful to Mark for having saved her at what seemed to have been the very last moment from his repulsive attentions.

Even to think of it made her feel again his strong arms pulling her against him, and see his lips seeking hers and his eyes burning with a fire that terrified her.

Mark had come into her life unexpectedly, but she had known on board the ship she was vividly aware of him as a commanding figure and a man of authority.

Yet at the same time, he was someone who could explain to her about love.

She had never known anyone like him, and it was hard to recognise in him as he was to-day the cousin who, as a boy, had teased her and whom she had hated because he had taken David from her side.

When dinner was over Cordelia excused herself to her hostess and retired to bed.

She thought as it was early that she would not sleep, but almost before she expected it she slipped away into a dreamless slumber to be awakened by Church bells.

She jumped out of bed feeling excited at how much more there was to see and do, and of all the many days that stretched ahead of her.

The Countess had promised that to-day she should meet the Grand Master von Hompesch, and that they would also visit the ramparts and the great Fort of St. Elmo.

It was all very exciting. At the same time Cordelia wanted more than anything else to see Mark and David.

'Surely they will visit me this morning?' she thought.

Almost as if her need of them communicated itself to their minds, she had hardly finished breakfast before Mark arrived.

She was so glad to see him that she sprang up from the table to run towards him impulsively the moment he was announced.

"I was hoping you would come!" she cried.

"I expect you would like to talk to your cousin alone," the Countess said. "Why do you not go into the garden-room where no-one will disturb you?"

Cordelia thanked her, and they went into a beautiful Sitting-Room at the back of the house which had large windows opening into a small flower-filled garden.

They sat down in comfortable chairs where what breeze there was came to them from off the sea.

"It is going to be very hot later," Mark said.

"Do you realise it is the 6th June to-day?" Cordelia asked. "One must expect great heat, especially in the Mediterranean."

"Of course," he agreed.

There was something in the way he spoke which told Cordelia his mind was on other matters.

"What is it?" she asked.

"I have wanted to talk to you, Cordelia," he said, "because it is important that we make arrangements for you to return to England as soon as possible."

"Why? Why?" she asked. "You have not said anything about this before."

Mark knew he had to choose his words with care.

He did not wish to explain to Cordelia that it was the inadequacy of Malta's defences which made him feel it imperative to get her away to safety.

"Have you decided with whom you will live when you return home?" he enquired.

"No," Cordelia replied. "David said there was no hurry for me to do that because I should be here with him for at least six months or a year."

"I do not think that is practical."

"But why? The Count and Countess seem only too pleased to have me. They have already said so, and if not, there are doubtless other people who would not object to having a guest who would pay her expenses."

"I do not want you to stay."

She looked at him, her grey eyes searching his blue ones, then said:

"I know you have a reason for saying that. Can it be possible that you think I might be in danger here?"

"I am not prepared to answer any questions," he replied. "It is just that I would like your permission, Cordelia, to arrange for you to travel on the first available ship that is going to England."

Cordelia gave a little laugh.

"I think in that case I shall very likely be here for a very long time. The Count said last night that most ships are afraid of travelling far from their own ports."

She paused, saw that Mark was not impressed, and went on:

"Besides I might be captured by one of the Barbary

Pirates. Surely you would not wish to think of me in prison in Algiers or Tangier?"

"I am serious about wishing you to leave, Cordelia."

"And I am equally serious in saying that I intend to stay." She put out her hand towards him.

"You have been very kind to me, Mark. I am deeply grateful for the way in which you saved me from the Duca. At the same time I want to stay in Malta and I intend to do so."

"You will find me very obstinate where you are concerned," Mark said, "and I promise you, Cordelia, I am thinking only of you."

"I think the truth is that you would be glad to be rid of such a tiresome encumbrance!"

She was laughing as she looked up into his eyes. Then quite unexpectedly they were both very still.

It was as if something passed between them, something strange and magnetic, something Cordelia could not explain, and yet it was there.

She felt almost as if Mark drew her nearer to him, and yet he had not moved.

She felt her heart begin to beat rather quickly, when suddenly the door burst open.

Cordelia turned her head expecting to see David, but it was Ludwig von Wütenstein who stood there.

"Captain Stanton," he began breathlessly, "I knew you were here and I have run all the way."

"What is it? What has happened?"

"We must put to sea immediately," the Baron gasped. "There is no time to be lost. It is an opportunity which may not come again."

"Supposing you explain a little more coherently?" Mark suggested.

"A ship of the Order has just arrived in port. It apprehended a Pirate Ship off the coast en route for Tunis. It contained a fabulous cargo of spices worth hundreds of scudis and they also took fifty prisoners!"

"That is good news!" Mark said. "But how does this affect us?"

"There were two Pirate Ships! Two! The *Santa Maria* had to let one get away," the Baron replied. "But she shot down its main mast and it will not be able to move quickly."

Mark did not speak and the Baron cried :

"Can you not see how easy it would be for us to apprehend it? And there is no other ship of the Order in the harbour ready to leave immediately as we are."

Mark smiled.

"Then it is obviously our duty not to allow the Pirates to get that cargo to safety."

"I knew you would agree – I knew it!" Ludwig cried excitedly.

He turned towards the door.

"I am going straight to the *St. Jude*. Will I meet you there?"

"Within a quarter of an hour," Mark replied.

The door slammed behind the young Baron and they heard him running along the corridor.

Mark turned to Cordelia.

"I am afraid our conversation must be postponed until my return."

"You will be away ... long?"

"I should imagine not more than a week, perhaps less," he answered. "Take care of yourself, Cordelia."

He put out his hand. As she took it she moved closer to him.

"And you must take care of . . . yourself. Will it be dangerous?"

"I will not tempt fate by answering that question," he replied with a smile.

Her fingers tightened on his.

"I wish you were not going," she said in a low voice. "I shall be . . . worried and . . . anxious all the time you are away."

"I want you to enjoy yourself, Cordelia, so forget about me."

"It will be ... difficult to do ... that."

She looked into his eyes and once again was held by some strange magic.

"Please . . . please be . . . careful!" she said in a voice that was little above a whisper.

For a moment Mark was very still. Then almost as if he could not help himself, as if it was inevitable, his arms went round her.

He pulled her close against him and his lips came down on hers.

It was a very gentle kiss such as a man might give a child, and her lips were soft beneath his.

Then Cordelia felt something strange and quite inexplicable happen within herself.

It was a feeling so rapturous, so marvellous, that for the moment she could hardly believe it was happening. It was a wonder she had never imagined possible.

It seemed to rise from her heart into her throat, then to her lips which Mark held captive.

It was a feeling so perfect that it was as if she kissed the sunlight, and it enveloped her.

Then, before she could be sure of it, almost before she could realise what it meant, he set her free.

"Good-bye, Cordelia."

She thought his voice was low and a little hoarse.

Then without looking at her again he walked from the room, closing the door quietly behind him.

Chapter Five

After Mark had left the room Cordelia stood staring at the door, as if she felt it held the answer to the turbulent feelings within her.

Instinctively her hands went to her breasts. Then she walked towards the window to look out with unseeing eyes at the small flower-filled garden.

She knew as if a voice from Heaven had spoken that this was love!

This was what she had been seeking. This was the realisation of her dream!

She had found the man who could bring her the love which had subconsciously been part of her thoughts although she had not been aware of it.

She had always known that when she found love it would be, as Mark had said, divine.

She felt herself quiver as she remembered and felt again the strange, inexpressible wonder he had aroused in her.

She had not known that a man's lips could be so firm and yet while he had held her captive she had not been afraid.

She admitted to herself that she had wanted him to go on kissing her, to feel the incredible enchantment of being close to him, of knowing that her whole being responded to an ecstasy that came from her heart.

"I love him!" she said in a voice that trembled.

She felt as if the sunshine was suddenly more brilliant, the flowers more colourful, the music of the birds and bees joining in a paean of joy.

This was love! It illumined the whole world and Heaven itself, and she knew that, as she had foreseen, she had grown from a child into a woman.

How long she stood there looking out into the garden she

had no idea. She only knew that a happiness not of this world enveloped her like an aura of light.

It was in fact not much later that the Countess came to find her and was surprised that she was alone.

"Has your cousin already left, Lady Cordelia?"

With an effort Cordelia managed to reply in what was almost a normal voice that Captain Stanton had been called away.

"Is there anything special you wish to do this morning?" the Countess enquired.

"I would like, if it is no trouble, to go to the shops," Cordelia answered. "I suspect that my brother will be too busy to visit me."

"I am sure he will," the Countess replied with a smile. "Novices find their time fully occupied. It is only when they have taken the vows and finished their 'caravans' that time lies heavy on their hands."

"How many Knights are there in Malta?" Cordelia enquired.

"About four hundred," the Countess replied, "but of those two hundred are French."

"As many as that? And the rest?"

"Italian, Spanish, Portuguese, Bavarian, and German," the Countess answered.

Cordelia did not say anything but she could not help feeling that if the rumours of war with Bonaparte were to be believed it would surely be extremely difficult for the French to fire on their own countrymen.

But she told herself she was being needlessly apprehensive when she walked with the Countess through the narrow crowded streets and climbed the long flights of stone steps overhung with balconies brilliant with flowers.

Everything seemed so peaceful that the mere idea of warfare of any sort in this glorious island seemed ridiculous.

Besides it was impossible not to be impressed by the massive fortifications which had been called 'bulky mountain-breasted heights', and the sharp-pointed bastions of St. Elmo, the glacis and the heavy draw-bridge of Porte des Bombes.

The shops were even more entrancing than they had seemed the first day she had visited them.

She bought a small present for her hostess which delighted the Countess and an ancient sword set with jewels that she thought would please David.

She wondered if she should buy anything for Mark, in fact she longed to do so.

Then she thought it might seem a little forward to give him a present and that no doubt his kiss, the magic of which still lingered on her lips, had not meant as much to him as it had to her.

And yet, she told herself, a kiss could only be perfect if two people felt the same.

Although she was very ignorant of love, she knew with some inner conviction which would not be denied that Mark had been moved when his lips touched hers.

"I love him! I love him!" she told herself a thousand times during the day.

After a light luncheon they all retired for the customary siesta, when the whole City went quiet and even the song of the birds seemed muted.

The Countess went to her bed-room to rest, but Cordelia lay on a *chaise longue* in the Sitting-Room which looked out onto the garden.

The shades were half drawn and the room was dim and cool.

She shut her eyes, but she did not sleep. She was thinking of Mark, remembering how handsome he was and how she had in fact, she recognised now, loved him before they left Naples.

She had thought that he annoyed her and that she disliked him.

But she knew after they had talked together in the garden and he had been so understanding and explained all that had perplexed her, that her heart had gone out to him.

"Can there be another man like him?" she asked.

So strong, so masculine, so essentially a man, and yet so understanding and gentle that it would have been impossible not to trust him and do anything that he asked of her.

She prayed for him and felt that her prayer winged its way across the sea.

She could imagine the *St. Jude* speeding over the white-crested waves and the pirate ship with its broken mast vainly trying to escape.

Although he would take prisoner the crew of cruel and usually brutal Moslems, Mark would show them the magnanimity and the kindness of which the Chaplain had spoken.

"I love him . . . he is everything that a man should be!" Cordelia told herself again. "And he behaves like a Knight even if he has not taken his vows."

She knew as she thought of it she was glad he had not done so, and the thought that he was free brought the colour to her cheeks and her heart beat a little faster.

Suddenly there was the sound of voices outside.

She could hear the Count speaking loudly in what seemed an agitated manner and a moment later the door of the Sitting-Room was thrown open and the Countess appeared, followed by her husband.

One glance at her hostess's face made Cordelia sit up quickly on the *chaise longue*.

"What is it?" she asked. "What has happened?"

"The French!" the Countess ejaculated.

Wide-eyed, Cordelia looked at the Count for confirmation.

"It is true, Lady Cordelia," he said. "The French Fleet have arrived!"

"What do they want of Malta?" Cordelia asked in a low voice.

"Water, I expect," the Count replied. "In fact I have been told that a launch from Bonaparte's ship *L'Orient* is already entering the Grand Harbour!"

Cordelia gave a little sigh of relief.

"That does not sound as if they intend to conquer the island."

"No, indeed," the Count agreed, "but I understand there is an Alert."

"Find out all you can," the Countess begged, "and if you think it is safe, Lady Cordelia and I will go on the roof to look at the ships."

"I cannot imagine that you will come to any harm there," the Count replied, "but you must keep out of the streets. There is sure to be a certain amount of panic amongst the poorer people in the town, and the mere name of Bonaparte is enough to send the women into hysterics!"

He walked from the room as he spoke and Cordelia rose from the *chaise longue*.

"I suppose there is no . . . chance of my seeing David?" she asked.

"If there is an Alert," the Countess replied, "they will all be at their dispositions for defence."

She gave a little sigh.

"My husband has said for years that Malta needed new guns. Many have been repeatedly painted to look like new, but they have only been used for ceremonial purposes."

"In Naples they talked of little else except war and Napoleon Bonaparte's ambitions," Cordelia said. "It seems strange that the Knights are not more prepared."

"Let us pray that they will not have to fight," the Countess exclaimed, "because I cannot help feeling that experienced French soldiers who have been victorious in so many campaigns already, will be formidable opponents."

When they reached the flat roof of the house Cordelia could only echo what the Countess had said.

From the roof-tops they had a spacious view of the sea. It was covered for miles with ships of all sizes whose masts resembled a huge forest.

It would have been a magnificent sight if it had not been so frightening.

There was no doubt that Bonaparte's Fleet contained the finest and newest men-o'-war and amongst them it was easy to distinguish a superb three-decker, *L'Orient*, the Flagship in which he travelled.

Cordelia and the Countess looked at the Fleet for some time but they said very little.

With grave expressions on their faces they went downstairs to await the Count's return.

When he arrived he looked extremely worried.

"What has happened? Tell us what you have discovered," the Countess said before he could speak.

"I was right," he replied. "Officers from *L'Orient* have asked the Grand Master to admit the Fleet for water. Von Hompesch has convened a Council for six o'clock and I am told by a friend in the Palace that the members will urge the Grand Master to enforce the regulation that only four ships can enter the Harbour at once."

"Surely, then it will take a very long time to supply the whole Fleet?" Cordelia said.

"That is what my friend thought," the Count replied. "And he pointed out that, if Bonaparte would agree to such a stipulation, it would allow time for the British to appear."

"The British?" the Countess exclaimed, clasping her hands together. "But we understood that they were blockading Toulon. Surely the French can not have defeated them in battle?"

She spoke in such an agitated manner that the Count put his arm around his wife's shoulder.

"Do not distress yourself, my dear, there has been no battle. My friend learnt from the Officer who came from *L'Orient* that the French Armada slipped out of Toulon when Nelson was watering his ships off *Sardinia!*"

He smiled a little wryly as he said :

"I was told the French are delighted at having hoodwinked the British, and are laughing about it rather like school-boys who have escaped their master's vigilance."

He paused before he added :

"The size of the Fleet is certainly intimidating; I am told that *L'Orient* alone carries a thousand men and one hundred and twenty guns."

The Countess gave a little cry and he finished :

"She has also £600,000 in sterling aboard."

The Count did not stay long and it was two hours after dinner had been served before he returned again.

As he had anticipated, the Council had, with only one

dissenting voice, that of a Spaniard, urged the Grand Master to enforce the regulations.

"Are you sure General Bonaparte will accept such a ruling?" the Countess asked in a worried voice.

The Count did not answer and Cordelia knew that he was calculating how long it would take to water so many ships.

It was impossible to sleep that night.

Cordelia found herself rising again and again to walk about her bed-chamber, worrying about David and worrying too in case Mark on the *St. Jude* had run into the French Fleet.

She thought it was unlikely because Napoleon's ships had sailed in from the north while Mark would have turned south towards the coast of Africa.

At the same time she had a horrifying feeling that a great drama was being played out around her and no-one could be certain of the outcome.

It was at dawn that Cordelia heard the sound of gunfire.

She dressed herself hastily and hurried downstairs to find the Countess up and learnt that the Count had already left the house to find out what was happening.

"I was sure, Lady Cordelia," the Countess said, "that Bonaparte would not wait so long for the water he requires."

"I was sure of it too," Cordelia replied. "If only we could know what is happening."

"We are not to leave the house," the Countess told her. "My husband left strict instructions that we were to stay here behind closed doors."

This, Cordelia thought, was harder to bear than anything else.

They could hear the noise in the streets outside, but they did not dare to disobey the Count and could only wait apprehensively, shuddering at the intermittent sound of gunfire.

"What can be happening?" the Countess asked again and again.

When finally the Count appeared she ran towards him with a cry, flinging her arms around him.

"You were so long and I was so afraid!" she exclaimed. "You are safe?"

"Quite safe," the Count replied. "But the whole place is in confusion and panic."

"What has happened?"

"As I expected," he replied, "Bonaparte has landed his forces on the Island."

The Countess gave a scream.

"I understand five battalions of Infantry landed at dawn in St. Julian's Bay," the Count went on. "They were opposed by fire from the Malta Regiment, who quickly retreated into Valetta."

He paused before he continued :

"I am not quite certain what happened next, but I was told that a number of French came ashore at Marsa Scirocco unopposed, under the command of General Marmont who cleared our sharp-shooters from Wignacourt's Aqueduct."

"But surely the Knights are fighting?" Cordelia asked breathlessly.

"It is difficult to be certain how much fighting there has actually been," the Count said in a tone that Cordelia felt was almost apologetic.

"There are large parties of Maltese soldiers behind the earth ramparts outside the walls of Floriana," he went on quickly. "I was told that the French were checked and that the Auvergnat Knights led a sally over the draw-bridge of the Porte des Bombes."

"It was successful?" Cordelia questioned.

"I am afraid not," the Count answered. "And General Marmont himself captured the Standard of the Order."

"I cannot believe it!" the Countess cried. "Surely our troops could not allow that to happen?"

"You must understand that these are only rumours, my dear," the Count said. "I have heard the reports which have reached the Grand Master at the Palace. But no-one will know for some hours whether or not they are true."

"And what is the Grand Master doing?" the Countess asked angrily.

The Count looked uncomfortable.

"You must tell me," his wife said insistently.

"Many of the leading people in the City and a number of

the nobles are meeting to aver that they have no confidence in the Order's powers to defend us. They wish to pass a resolution calling on the Grand Master to come to terms with Bonaparte."

"No! No!" the Countess cried. "It is too shaming! It would be a disgrace which will go down in history! You cannot – you must not allow yourself to be a party to such a resolution!"

"I must do what my conscience tells me is right," the Count said with dignity.

He patted his wife's arm in an effort at reassurance and said:

"I only returned so that I could tell you what was happening. I must go at once to be with our own people and help them determine what is best for Malta."

"Be strong, please, my dear. Be strong!" the Countess begged.

"What with?" the Count asked bitterly. "I have been told that the powder for the guns has been found to be rotten and the shot defective!"

The Countess gave a cry of sheer horror.

"The streets are full of our people," he went on, "cursing the French and the Grand Master at the same time, and imploring the Saints to preserve the Island! I have been told that the French Knights have refused to fire on their countrymen."

"It might have been expected," Cordelia said.

But when the Count had left the house and the Countess wept, she found it hard to keep her self-control.

At the same time she knew that nothing could be gained by collapsing or becoming as panic-stricken as those who were in the streets outside.

"David will expect me to be brave," she told herself.

She knew too that she could not bear Mark to think her a coward.

"Should we not cut up some linen for bandages?" she suggested to the Countess. "If there are wounded, bandages will be very necessary and perhaps the Hospital will not have sufficient supplies."

As if she was glad of something to do, the Countess agreed.

She produced some linen sheets which they cut into strips and rolled neatly, putting them in baskets so that they were ready as soon as they were required.

It grew later and later but there was no sign of the Count, and finally the Countess insisted that Cordelia should go to bed.

"You can do nothing now, Lady Cordelia," she said, "and if our services are required to-morrow, we shall be of little use if we are heavy-eyed and too exhausted to be of any assistance."

It was common sense, Cordelia thought, and finally she allowed herself to be persuaded to go to her bed-room.

Perhaps because her anxiety had left her more exhausted than she realised she actually slept for some hours.

At dawn she dressed again and crept quietly down the stairs so as not to arouse anyone else in the household.

She had reached the hall when she heard a knock at the front door.

The Count's establishment was not large enough to include a night-watchman, and it was so early that Cordelia was certain the servants were not yet awake.

The knock came again.

Although she was certain the Countess would think it somewhat reprehensible, Cordelia drew back the bolts on the door and turned the heavy key in the lock.

Outside she saw Vella.

Her heart gave a frightened leap. Then she opened the door a little wider and he stepped into the hall.

"What is it?" Cordelia whispered. "Has anything happened to His Lordship?"

"I came to you as soon as I could, Mistress," Vella said.

"What has happened?" Cordelia asked.

She knew even as she spoke by the expression on the servant's face what he had to tell her.

"The Master is – dead!"

With an effort Cordelia opened the nearest door and entered a Sitting-Room.

She sat down on a chair feeling as if her legs would no longer hold her. Then with her eyes on the face of the Maltese she said quietly :

"Tell me what . . . happened."

"The Master was very brave," Vella said in a low voice. "He was with two Auvergnat Knights who attacked the French over the draw-bridge of the Porte des Bombes."

He took a deep breath.

"I was with him, Mistress, and while some of the troops were reluctant to put up any opposition, the Master was insistent that they must fight."

Cordelia could almost see David with the light of a visionary in his eyes, exhorting the soldiers and being determined to oppose the French.

"The French boats laden with soldiers drew nearer the Porte, Mistress. They were led, I understand, by General Marmont himself."

Almost before he could say the words Cordelia knew what had happened.

"There was some cross-fire," Vella went on. "Then the General made to capture the Standard of the Order."

Cordelia drew in her breath.

"It was then that the Master would have rushed at him with his sword."

"What happened then?" Cordelia whispered.

"The General raised his own sword to defend himself, but one of the soldiers in the boats shot at the Master and hit him in the chest. He fell backwards, and as he fell he cried : 'For Christ and for the Order!' "

Cordelia felt the tears come into her eyes. Impatiently she brushed them away.

"Where is he now, Vella?"

"I had to wait until nightfall, Mistress, to find someone to help me, but I have taken his body to the Church of St. John."

"Will you take me there?" Cordelia asked.

The Maltese nodded and she rose to her feet.

There was a cupboard in the Hall which held coats and capes. She opened the door and took out the first cape she could find.

It covered her gown and she pulled the hood over her head.

Vella shut the front door behind them and they set off in the pale light of dawn.

The streets in the neighbourhood of the Manduca house were empty. But as they drew nearer to the more populous part of the town there were already small crowds gathered at the street corners.

"Yesterday, Mistress," Vella said, "the Churches were crowded to the doors with terrified people praying for a miracle."

"I can understand their fears," Cordelia murmured.

"The corridors and Courts of the Magisterial Palace were a surging mass of Knights," Vella went on, "and everywhere there was uproar and conflicting rumours."

"I understand that the French Knights refused to fight."

"I think that was true, Mistress. But a number of Maltese soldiers lost their lives, although I was told that some threw down their arms and ran away!"

Cordelia gave a little gasp but said nothing. All she could think of was that David was dead.

It was not a long walk to the Church of St. John, but she felt as if it had taken hours.

At last she saw the two bell towers and they passed through the central door into the nave.

There was the sweet scent of incense and the flicker of the sanctuary lights. Then as she walked over the colourful tablets of jewelled mosaic beneath which the Knights lay buried, she saw lying in the Chancel the body of a man.

She knew it was David before she reached him.

Vella had laid him down with his face towards the high altar and his two hands clasped over his sword which lay upon his breast.

The pale morning light coming through the stained-glass windows seemed to touch David's fair hair with a finger of gold as if it haloed his head.

Cordelia went down on her knees.

It seemed almost unbelievable that David should be dead. His eyes were closed, he appeared to be asleep.

Then she saw that his face held an expression of almost radiant happiness.

There was a smile on his lips, and she knew that if she could have seen his eyes they would have held that visionary light which came into his face whenever he spoke of his faith.

For a long time she looked at him.

Then as instinctively the beautiful words of the Prayer for the Dead came to her lips, Cordelia knew that David was not dead, but alive.

He had joined the Knights whose presence she had felt when she first came to the Church, and now he was in their company, with his faith, by which he had lived and for which he had died, untarnished as theirs had been.

David had found his dream and he had not been disappointed.

Cordelia reached out her hand and touched his, finding it strange that it should be cold while he still seemed so alive.

Then as she raised her face to the cross on the Altar, she knew there was no death, only life, and David was still living out his vows.

Vella touched her shoulder.

"We must go, Mistress," he said. "It is getting late and it may not be safe for you to be in the streets."

Cordelia rose to her feet and took one last look at her brother. Then she moved away, leaving him among the effigies of other Knights who had fought for Christ and St. John.

They moved through the streets quickly.

Occasionally Cordelia had a glimpse of bands of French soldiers in the distance, but Vella hurried her down side-alleys and up steep narrow steps, so that they would not be seen.

They were within sight of the Count's house when Cordelia stopped and faced the Maltese beside her.

"Vella," she said insistently, "we must warn Captain Stanton."

He looked at her in surprise.

"He is not on the Island, Mistress."

"I am aware of that," Cordelia replied. "He left yesterday morning taking his ship to intercept a pirate vessel carrying a cargo to Tunis. He did not expect to be away for long; but if he returns and the French are still here, they will confiscate the ship even if they do not fire at it!"

Vella listened intently, then he said:

"It might be possible, Mistress, to intercept the Captain. I could find out in the harbour exactly where he has gone."

"And you could obtain a boat so that it would be possible to warn him what has occurred in Malta?"

Vella thought for a moment, then said:

"It will cost money, Mistress."

"That is no problem," Cordelia replied. "I have quite a large sum in cash, I also have some jewellery."

As Vella did not speak she said with a note of resolution in her voice:

"You must get the best boat you can, Vella, because I intend to go with you!"

"You, Mistress? But that would be dangerous!"

"That does not trouble me," Cordelia said quickly. "What is important is for us to warn Captain Stanton. Whatever happens he must not return to Malta until the French have left; and if they take over the Island it will still be dangerous!"

Vella nodded as if he understood.

Cordelia was thinking quickly.

"I will go back to the house now," she said. "It is unlikely that anyone will be awake. I will give you what money I have, and my jewellery to sell. When you have done that and found out all you can in the harbour regarding Captain Stanton's movements, come and tell me what arrangements you have made."

"I will do that, Mistress."

There was a note in Vella's quiet voice and the way he spoke which told Cordelia she could trust him.

* * *

It was after midnight when Cordelia finally left the Count's house, and everyone, she was sure, was fast asleep after the agitations and anxieties of the day.

The Count himself was hoarse with tiredness, as he told his wife, from arguing in the Magisterial Palace and attempting to put the Maltese point of view to the Grand Master.

Von Hompesch had done nothing but dither, being swayed first by this argument, then by that, and finding it impossible to make up his mind what to do one way or another.

Finally he did nothing, and reports that the Knights had surrendered the Island to the French gained conviction with every passing hour.

There were rumours of desertion and disobedience mixed with confusion; stories of Knights being killed or dangerously wounded and of fights in which those in the crowd were stabbed or bludgeoned.

Finally white flags were raised over St. Elmo and Fort Ricasoli and von Hompesch prepared to receive Napoleon's Emissaries in the Council Chamber.

Without the waste of many words a twenty-four hour truce was signed on condition that the Grand Master should send his Plenipotentiaries to negotiate the surrender of the Island.

"The representatives included four Maltese," the Count said in answer to a question from his wife, "and they have already left on the three-mile journey to *L'Orient* by launch."

Having reported what he knew up to date, the Count had retired to bed and Cordelia told them that she intended to do the same thing.

The Countess had been very sympathetic and understanding about David's death, but Cordelia found it difficult to speak about it.

She was determined not to yield to her natural impulse to break down in a passion of weeping, until she was sure that she had saved Mark.

She felt frantically that she could not lose the man she loved as well as her beloved brother.

It was strange, she used to think afterwards, that she had trusted Vella so implicitly that she never for one moment questioned that he would do as she asked of him.

She had given him all her money and all her jewellery,

some of which was worth a considerable amount.

It included a pearl necklace which had belonged to her mother, two diamond brooches and a diamond bracelet which she had inherited.

Even allowing for the fact that the traders would be upset by the confusion caused by the arrival of the French, there was no reason to think they would not appreciate the value of the fine diamonds.

Vella had promised to come to her as soon after midnight as was possible, and long before the hour struck in a dozen Church towers Cordelia crept downstairs.

She had put on her riding boots and was wearing the dark cloak which she had borrowed to go to the Church of St. John earlier in the day.

Vella's knock on the door was very faint.

She opened it immediately and they neither of them spoke for fear of being overheard. Vella closed the door behind them and they hurried away from the vicinity of the house.

Cordelia had already written a long letter of explanation to the Countess, telling her that she had gone to find Mark, but not saying where he had gone, for fear the letter might fall into French hands and they would be intercepted.

In the shadows at the end of the street Vella had waiting for her two ponies. They were 'Barbs' which came from the Barbary Coast and were always ridden by the Maltese.

They were held by a small ragged boy who accepted a few coins for his trouble and at once disappeared. Cordelia and Vella set off at a sharp pace, finding it easy to see the way by the light of the moon in the starlit sky.

"You have a boat?" Cordelia asked after they had gone a short distance.

"My cousin has a caïque, Mistress, in the south of the island. He is anxious that we should reach him with all possible speed as he wishes to set out to sea before daylight."

Cordelia knew that this was in order to avoid the French ships.

At the same time as the majority of them were anchored in the vicinity of Valetta, the south coast of the island might, she reasoned, be almost clear of enemy vessels.

They were soon away from the City and now they were passing through vineyards and olive groves.

The Knights, Cordelia had heard from the Count, had introduced many new industries during their reign in Malta, but agriculture employed more men and women than any other.

They skirted fields growing grain and cotton and avoided the barren lime-stone hills.

They rode through small villages in which there were large herds of goats and Cordelia could not help thinking that a large number of them, together with pigs and sheep, would be slaughtered to victual the French ships.

Everywhere peasants and thrifty farmers suffered in time of war, she thought bitterly, and Napoleon's Armies wherever they fought had always lived off the land.

They rode fast, Vella leading the way so that all Cordelia had to do was to follow him.

She was glad that she was a proficient horse-woman and that it did not tire her unduly to be in the saddle for a long time.

Finally, when the stars were fading and the moon was almost indiscernible in the sky, she saw the sea ahead.

Avoiding the fortifications they moved along narrow, twisting paths until finally they reached the shore.

The Maltese had always burrowed into the lime-stone of their island, and after they had moved a little way along a gravelly beach Cordelia could see the outline of the bow of a boat half-hidden in a roughly hewn cave.

Men came to greet them and she was introduced to Vella's cousin, a short, stocky-looking man like himself, dressed as a fisherman but speaking in a more cultured manner than his appearance would suggest.

The cousins talked together for some minutes and there was an exchange of money. Then Vella made a gesture to Cordelia that she should go aboard.

A boy appeared from nowhere to take their horses.

Carrying a little bundle under her arm which comprised all the possessions Cordelia had brought with her, she was helped into a boat which was rocking gently on the waves.

She saw at once that it was larger than she had expected and realised it was a caïque of the type used along the shores of the Mediterranean by the natives of every country.

She counted a crew of seven, which, with herself and Vella as passengers, made a complement of nine.

Then speaking in low voices the seamen took the boat into the open sea, having muffled the long oars to deaden the sound.

As Cordelia felt the waves slap against the wooden sides and as the crew started to raise the big sail, she felt with a little throb of excitement, that she had succeeded!

She could hardly believe it possible that her impulsive idea of saving Mark and of warning him that the French were in Malta could be an actuality.

When she had pretended to go to bed in the Count's house, she had felt it was a hundred to one chance against her being able to get away from the island.

Vella might not be able to sell the jewellery, his cousin might refuse to hire the boat, they might be intercepted before they reached the coast.

There were dozens of things which might have happened to prevent her getting away.

And yet unbelievably everything had gone smoothly.

Now the only difficulty was to find Mark and as far as they themselves were concerned to avoid the French.

The sea was choppy and Cordelia was thankful that she never yet in her life had been sea-sick. She had been in some very rough storms, but she had found them invigorating and had never succumbed as most women did.

Vella came to her side.

"It is a good boat, Mistress," he said as if he must justify the expense, "and my cousin is a very fine navigator."

"You have found out where Captain Stanton is likely to be?" Cordelia asked.

"I saw the pilot of the *St. Maria* who had brought the cargo captured from the pirates into the Grand Harbour."

"What will happen to the cargo now?" Cordelia asked, thinking as she spoke that it was a somewhat senseless question.

"The French are very avaricious, Mistress," Vella said quietly.

Cordelia thought of all the wonderful treasures that Valetta contained.

"If the French take possession of Malta, what will become of the Knights' property?" she asked herself. "Those fabulous pictures and furniture, tapestries and historical relics?"

Then she thought reassuringly that the Grand Master would doubtless make some provision for them in the terms of surrender.

But the stories she had heard of Bonaparte's ruthlessness and the manner in which he had extorted the last penny from those whom he conquered were not very encouraging.

The caïque was heading north west, but once or twice in the darkness she saw the grey outlines of great ships and their masts were silhouetted against the sky.

But if they noticed the caïque, the French look-outs must have thought it was only a fishing-boat and they passed unchallenged.

Slowly the sable of the night faded and an hour later there was the first pale gold finger of the dawn in the east.

Cordelia looked back.

The Island of Malta was just a purple smudge on the horizon.

'It belongs to yesterday,' she thought. 'It is the past! Ahead lies to-morrow!'

Chapter Six

Cordelia ate the food which Vella offered her. It was only coarse almost black bread and the goat's milk cheese which all the Maltese housewives made.

She was touched to find he had also brought fruit, obviously for her only, as she noticed that none of the seamen on board ate it.

There was red Maltese wine to drink which was sweet and not very strong.

The food took away the feeling of emptiness which she had felt since she awoke. She had been too agitated to eat any dinner last night and after David's death her luncheon had gone untouched.

It was Vella who, once dawn had come, persuaded her to lie down in the small cabin below and try to sleep.

There she found a hard bunk covered with blankets which were old and faded. Yet the place was clean and Cordelia, having taken off her riding boots and her cloak, made herself comfortable.

She slept although she was certain she would be too anxious to do so.

"We will keep watch for the *St. Jude*, Mistress," Vella said, "and tell you the moment she is sighted."

Because she did in fact feel very tired after the long night, Cordelia did as he suggested and when she awoke the sun was high in the heavens and it was already afternoon.

It was also very hot and Cordelia was glad when she came on deck that it was possible to find shade under the big sail.

The wind was still behind them and they were therefore moving swiftly, but as the afternoon progressed she began to feel worried that they might have missed Mark and that he had returned to Malta by the route to the west of Gozo.

The sea seemed limitless and where the horizon met the sky there was only a blending of colour without a mast in sight.

Cordelia began to wonder how soon it would be if they did not find Mark before she was forced to tell the caïque to turn back towards Malta.

The seamen in charge of the boat smoked when they were not attending to the sails and rigging and frequently spat into the sea.

They were all dark-skinned Maltese, their faces lined and weather-beaten, their eyes bright and alert.

She was well aware that now the French were in possession it might be extremely unpleasant for her, being English.

It was different for the Countess who was married to a Maltese, but to be an enemy of France and in the power of Bonaparte at this moment was something too unpleasant to contemplate.

Vella was standing in the bow of the boat looking out to sea.

Suddenly he gave a shout.

"What is it?" Cordelia asked quickly.

"A mast! I can see a mast on the starboard bow!"

The man at the tiller of the caïque altered course to starboard and Cordelia felt that she was unable to breathe before Vella gave another shout that seemed to be echoed in the slap of the sails.

"I can see the Cross of the Order!" he cried. "'Tis the St. Jude!"

Cordelia clasped her hands together.

Now that Mark was sighted she realised how afraid she had been that she would not find him and that she had done the wrong thing in not waiting for his return.

She tried to see the St. Jude for herself, but when she attempted to stand up in the caïque it went about and she was almost swept overboard. Hastily she sat down again.

It took some time to cross the intervening sea between

themselves and Mark's ship, but at last they could see quite clearly the great eight-pointed Cross embellished on the sails which were however, half reefed in.

As they drew nearer still Cordelia realised that the ship was drifting with another vessel secured alongside.

"They are taking the cargo aboard, Mistress," Vella explained.

Now Cordelia could see that the pirate ship was secured to the *St. Jude* by grappling-irons and not only its main mast was broken but the other two were trailing over its side in the sea.

It was obvious that the *St. Jude*'s men were moving the cargo from the captured ship into their own hold.

In the stern were the Moslem prisoners, huddled together dejectedly, their hands on top of their heads as they were guarded by one of the soldiers of the Order.

At last Cordelia could see Mark moving about the deck giving orders, and even at a distance she could sense his air of authority.

Her heart had leapt at the sight of him and she found it difficult to look at anything else.

All through the night her love for him had seemed to encompass her like a protective wall, and now she knew she had been certain that somehow in some magical way she would find him and save him from the French.

At last they were within hailing distance. Vella was gesticulating wildly and shouting at the top of his voice:

"Cap-a-tain Stanton! Cap-a-tain Stanton! We bring – news!"

Cordelia saw a sailor draw Mark's attention to their approach and he came to the rail of the ship.

When he saw who was aboard the caïque she saw the astonishment on his face.

A rope-ladder was lowered over the side of the *St. Jude* and Cordelia was helped aboard, but not before she had thanked the owner and his men.

Vella himself came up the ladder after her, guiding her feet and helping her until Mark leant over the side and taking her arms pulled her to safety.

For a moment he held her close against him as he said in an incredulous tone:

"Cordelia! In God's name, what are you doing here?"

"I came to . . . warn you," she answered.

It was hard to speak because the mere fact that she was close to Mark and he had his arms around her made her quiver.

When her eyes met his it was hard to remember what she had to say.

"To warn me?" he questioned.

"The French have taken Malta!"

She saw the consternation in his expression and added: "David has been . . . killed!"

His hand clasped her closely as if in consolation. Then he said:

"The whole French Fleet is there?"

Cordelia nodded.

"Then Admiral Nelson cannot have received the communication I sent him from Naples," he said almost beneath his breath.

"The Count heard that the French had slipped out of Toulon while the British Fleet was being watered in Sardinia," Cordelia explained.

"That would account for it," Mark said. "But what is happening on the Island? Surely they are fighting?"

"There is very . . . little," Cordelia replied in a low voice. "The French Knights would not attack their own countrymen . . . and the defences were . . . inadequately manned."

She spoke unhappily, feeling it shaming that she should bring him such tidings. Then almost abruptly he said:

"This alters things considerably."

He walked away from her and she saw him speaking to the Baron and several other Officers who were supervising the removal of the cargo.

Without hearing what they said it was easy to discern their consternation and dismay at the news.

"Is all the cargo aboard?" Cordelia heard Mark ask.

"Only a dozen more bags, Sir," a Petty-Officer replied, "and of course the prisoners."

"We will take no prisoners!"

Cordelia saw the surprise on the faces of those who heard Mark. Then he called the Officer in charge of the pirate ship and speaking slowly and clearly so that he could understand he said:

"We have taken the cargo which you had stolen already from another ship, but we do not intend to take you or your men prisoners."

There was a look of puzzled astonishment on the Moslem's face as he repeated:

"No prisoners, Captain?"

"By the mercy of God you are free!" Mark Stanton said. "But remember in your turn to show mercy to those you capture."

The Moslem Officer seemed too stunned to reply and Mark gave the order to release the grappling-irons and hoist the sails.

He came back to Cordelia's side.

"Where are we going?" she asked.

"To Naples," he replied. "If we come in contact with the British Fleet on the way we can tell Admiral Nelson where the French are at this moment."

His eyes were hard as he said:

"I told the Grand Master that Bonaparte would be making for Egypt, and that Malta was the obvious place where he would require water."

"He did not believe you?" Cordelia asked.

"De Rohan said on his death-bed that he would be the last Grand Master to reign in Malta," Mark said, "and the Hospitallers believed that the end would come when there was a German at the head of the Order. Like so many old prophecies this one has come true!"

He walked away before Cordelia could answer.

The Baron came to her side. She felt he was half aware of what she had to tell him before she said in a low voice:

"David was . . . killed trying to save the Standard of the Order from the French."

"I am sorry, Lady Cordelia! I am terribly sorry."

"It was as he would have . . . wished to . . . die," Cordelia said and turned away so that the Baron would not see the tears in her eyes.

Because she knew Mark was busy and she did not wish to be a nuisance, she went below to the cabin she had occupied on the journey from Naples to Malta.

She thought how happy they had all been then and how to David every mile they travelled brought him nearer to his 'Promised Land'.

It was hard to believe that she would never see him again, and yet she had known when she knelt beside him in the Church of St. John that his spirit would never die.

They had been at sea for over an hour before Mark came below and she heard him knock on her cabin door.

She opened it and he came inside to stand.

The evening sun shining through the port-hole illuminated her fair hair and encompassed her with an almost unearthly radiance.

They stood looking at each other; then quite simply Mark held out his arms and she ran towards him.

Because she was shy she hid her face against his shoulder.

"I am sorry about David," he said gently. "It was brave of you — more courageous than I can possibly tell you — to come to warn me."

His arms tightened as he said:

"Vella has told me it was entirely your idea and how you planned it all. Could anyone be more wonderful?"

Cordelia felt herself tremble at what he said and the deep note in his voice.

"Look at me, my darling," Mark said.

But when she would have raised her face shyly towards his, knowing that he was about to kiss her and longing for the touch of his lips, there was a sudden shout.

"Sail ho! Sail ho!"

The voice seemed to ring out over their heads and without even a word of apology Mark took his arms from her and hurried from the cabin up the companionway to the deck.

Cordelia followed him.

She moved much more slowly than he did, and by the

time she stepped out into the sunshine he was already on the bridge and looking as was every other man on deck towards the horizon.

It was undoubtedly a sail, a dark mark against the sky. But it was too far away to see if it was friend or foe.

The lookout was clinging to his perch, being swung round and round in dizzy circles as the ship swooped over the waves.

Vella came to Cordelia's side.

"You did not wish to go back with your cousin?" she asked him.

He shook his head.

"I would wish to serve Captain Stanton and of course you, Mistress."

"I am very grateful to you for bringing me to the *St. Jude*," Cordelia said.

"The Captain has thanked me," Vella replied, "and Mistress, I have some money for you and also the string of pearls. It was not necessary to sell all your jewels."

He held out the pearls as he spoke and Cordelia took them from him and fastened them around her neck.

"I am glad to keep them, Vella, they belonged to my mother."

"I got a good price for the diamonds, Mistress," Vella said a little boastfully.

"You have been very clever," Cordelia replied.

But her eye went instinctively towards the ship which now was a little clearer.

It was a three-master, she saw, but it was impossible to tell at this distance what flag it carried.

Mark was in consultation with his Officers on the poop and she felt he must be apprehensive.

Was the approaching ship bigger than they were, and would the fact that they carried a heavy cargo weigh against them in a battle?

A battle!

Cordelia felt as if a sword pierced her heart at the thought. Suppose having lost David she should now lose Mark?

She longed to run to his side and ask for his reassurance.

She wished that he had kissed her as she knew he was about to do before he had been recalled to his duty.

The ship was coming nearer.

"Man the braces!" Mark shouted. "Beat to quarters and clear for action!"

As the drum rolled, the ship was in a turmoil of activity: guns were run out, the decks sanded, the hoses rigged to the pumps, the bulkheads taken down.

Then as if Mark suddenly realised Cordelia's presence he said sharply:

"Please go below, Lady Cordelia, and stay there! Whatever happens, do not come up on deck!"

It was an order and Cordelia obeyed it.

She went to her cabin, feeling how useless it was to be a woman in time of war.

It seemed to her as if hours passed before anything happened.

It was agony to sit alone in her cabin and not know if the ship which must now be clearly in sight of those on deck was French or English.

If it was English, she thought, it might be possible for Admiral Nelson to save Malta from French occupation.

If it was French, what would happen to them?

Suddenly without any warning the guns were fired in a rolling crash that shook the *St. Jude* to her keel.

Cordelia was deafened by it.

A voice she thought was Mark's shouted: "Stand by to go about!"

She could hear the voices of the ship's boys as they came running up from below with new charges for the guns.

She knew the Maltese crew would be thrusting wet swabs down the bore to extinguish any residual fragments of smouldering cartridge, ramming in the fresh shot and then the charges and heaving the guns up into firing positions again.

"Cock your locks!" Mark's voice ordered. "Take your aim. Fire!"

The roar of the broadside was deafening and coincided with the guns of the enemy.

The *St. Jude* was enveloped in smoke and there was the sound of rigging tumbling onto the deck.

Another salvo roared, vibrated and shook the ship.

Now there was a wholehearted cheer and Cordelia knew without being able to see what was happening that the enemy must have been hit, probably carrying away a mast.

Another salvo and yet another with the enemy firing in return, but she had an idea that most of the shots went wide of their target.

One however, must have hit the *St. Jude* because Cordelia felt the violent impact of it and she was almost thrown from the bed on which she had been sitting.

Yet another salvo appeared to silence the enemy ship and again there was a tremendous cheer.

Cordelia longed to defy Mark's orders and go up on deck, but she was afraid of angering him should she do so.

She did however go to the bottom of the companion-way to listen, hoping she could hear what was happening.

There were orders being given in quick staccato tones, the sound of bare feet running over the deck.

Then as she listened, again there was that clarion-cry of: 'Sail ho!'

There was almost complete silence for a moment. Then she heard Mark give orders but could not understand their significance.

She had the feeling however that this new ship meant danger and, if it was another French ship, then they were likely to be in trouble, especially as she was sure they had received one if not more hits during the engagement just ended.

She opened the door of the cabin on the starboard side and wondered why she had not thought of doing so before.

Now she could see through the port-hole the ship they had been fighting: there was no doubt that it was French and that they had damaged it considerably.

The masts were down, the sails dragging in the water, and far away though she was, Cordelia could see bodies of men who had been killed lying about on the deck.

They had struck their colours in surrender and Cordelia

felt that it was some compensation for the surrender of the Fort of St. Elmo.

But the *St. Jude* was moving away.

She knew the men were setting full sail, to catch all the wind possible to carry them out of reach of the on-coming ship.

It was as if everyone aboard the *St. Jude* was straining every nerve and muscle, Cordelia thought, to avoid danger.

Yet she knew with a perception which was unshakable that the ship was approaching swiftly and it might be impossible for them to escape.

There was nothing more to be seen from the port-hole since they were now out of sight of the stricken vessel and there were only the waves, gold and crimson in the setting sun.

Restlessly Cordelia walked back to her cabin.

If only Vella would come and tell her what was happening, she thought. If only she dared defy Mark and go up on deck and see for herself.

Then frighteningly although from some distance, there was the report of cannon-shot.

It must have fallen short of the *St. Jude* but Cordelia felt the ship alter course.

There was another salvo and another, and she knew the reason there was no answering fire from the *St. Jude* was that the approaching ship was out of range of their smaller guns.

She could remember David asking if the guns they carried were large enough for the new French vessels being built at Toulon, and she could remember Mark's reply.

These French ships they were encountering must be part of Napoleon's new Fleet and were hurrying to join him at Malta.

If that was so, then the *St. Jude* would be out-gunned and not even Mark's expertise and brilliant seamanship could save them from destruction.

Cordelia covered her face with her hands and even as she did so the whole ship shook from the impact of another cannon-shot.

At the same time *St. Jude* lifted to the recoil of her own guns and Cordelia's ears felt they were split with the sound of the broadside. Then came the enemy's crashing reply.

She heard the thunderous cracking as the rigging was shot away, one of the masts fell and the thud of the sails as they crashed onto the deck.

After that there was an inferno of sound in which she could distinguish little except an occasional human scream above the roar of the guns, the rat-tat of musket fire, the breaking of wood and the answering salvo from the *St. Jude*.

The guns were firing as often as they could be loaded but, although Cordelia listened, there was no shout of delight as appeared invariably at the fall of an enemy mast.

The firing went on and on until her head seemed to reel with it and she felt deafened with the agonising impact of its thunder upon her ear-drums.

Finally there was silence, a silence so ominous and so frightening that Cordelia could not believe it.

She hoped it was her hearing that was at fault, but knew it was more terrifying than that.

Finally, feeling as if she had passed through a special hell of her own and was surprised to find herself alive, she crept from her cabin and tentatively climbed the companionway.

As she emerged on deck she gave a gasp of sheer horror for it seemed as if it was a place of the dead and no-one was left alive.

All three masts of the *St. Jude* had been shot down, the mizzen-mast having snapped off nine feet from the deck.

Masts and yards and sails and rigging trailed alongside and astern.

Coils of rope were lying in an indescribable tangle and beneath them and the sails she knew men were lying either dead or stunned by their fall.

As she moved a little further from the companion-way she looked up onto the poop and her heart stood still.

She could see Mark lying on the deck. Beside him lay the Baron and several other Officers.

Cordelia ran up the steps.

Mark was lying with his back against the side, his legs stretched out in front of him, and one of them was a mass of blood!

She thought for a moment that he must be dead.

Then she told herself he was unconscious, and if she did not do something about his leg he would bleed to death.

The men around him seemed to be in the same predicament.

The Baron she could see had been hit in the chest and his coat was already crimson.

One of the other Officers was moaning, and Cordelia saw in horror that his hand had been practically blown away and was but a mangled mass of flesh and bone without shape to it.

For a moment she felt everything swim in front of her eyes, then she told herself that she was needed and that if she was to save anyone's life she must work speedily.

She turned to leave the bridge and took one last glance as she did so to where silhouetted against the sunset was the French ship that had destroyed them.

She was picking up survivors from the other vessel, but Cordelia realised that the *St. Jude* was drifting from them out of gunshot.

Hurriedly she went below to pull the sheets from the beds in the cabins.

She had an armful of them when she heard a step behind her and turned to see Vella.

"Vella, help me!"

She saw his hands were trembling but his voice was quite steady as he said:

"Give me the sheets, Mistress, I will tear them for you."

"Thank you, Vella."

He must have hidden somewhere safe while the battle was raging and she was thankful that he at least was unharmed.

She went back on deck and put a tourniquet on Mark's leg above the knee.

She was tightening it when he opened his eyes.

He looked at her and she thought that for the moment he

did not realise who she was, as he asked weakly:

"Are – we – afloat?"

"Yes," Cordelia answered.

He shut his eyes again as if the effort had been too much, and now Vella helped her pull off his stocking and she bandaged the terrible open wound in his leg.

She wondered as she did so if she would be able to save his leg or whether he would lose it.

She thought how he would hate to be a cripple, but it was better than being dead.

"We must release the tourniquet in about fifteen minutes," she said to Vella, and saw that the linen with which she had bandaged him was already crimson.

She moved to the side of the Baron.

She thought at first glance that he was dead. Then when Vella had helped her to pull off his coat she realised that he had only been struck in the shoulder.

"A sharp-shooter, Mistress," Vella said, "not cannon."

"The bullet must still be there," Cordelia said automatically.

But there was nothing she could do except try to stop the bleeding and make the Baron comfortable.

He was semi-conscious and groaning.

Vella fetched a pillow from one of the cabins on which he could rest his head.

Cordelia lost count after that of how many men she bandaged and how many men she and Vella pulled from under the sails, some of whom had suffered nothing worse than being hit violently on the head by the wreckage as it fell.

All the time the ship was swinging in the seas and as dusk fell Cordelia realised that the sea was rougher than it had been earlier in the day.

Now the seas were splashing over the sides soaking the wounded men in their spray, and Cordelia was also wet through as she tended them.

She kept going back to Mark to release the tourniquet and the last time she had done so he was conscious.

"You – should – not be – doing – this," he said with difficulty.

"I am unhurt and so is Vella," she answered. "If we tend the men now we can save the lives of many of them."

She did not tell him that she had spent much time bandaging men who had died before she could do any more for them.

Where a man's limb had been hit by a cannon-ball it was dirty, and remembering what her mother had told her Cordelia sent Vella below to find some spirit.

"It is easier to die from dirt and infection than from the wound itself," Lady Stanton had said in her soft voice. "I have been told that Admiral Nelson used raw spirit on the men who were wounded in his ships and saved many lives that way."

When Vella had found what was required, because she was certain it was important, Cordelia undid Mark's bandages, poured raw spirit over the terrible wound on his leg and dressed it with new bandages.

The pain brought him back to consciousness and he gave a cry before his self-control forced no more sound from his lips.

"I am sorry, Mark," Cordelia said, "but it will at least prevent the wound from becoming gangrenous."

Mark did not reply and she knew he was biting on his lip. Then he held out his hand towards the bottle of brandy and when Vella passed it to him he drank from it.

"There is – wine – below," he said in a hoarse voice. "Give – the men as – much as they can – drink. It will – dull – their – suffering."

"I should have thought of that," Cordelia said and continued bandaging.

A little while later Vella staggered up on deck carrying a dozen bottles at a time to distribute to all the men capable of using their hands.

The guns' crews on the lower deck also required Cordelia's attention.

The atmosphere below was stiffling. There was the bitter

smell of powder from the guns, the stink of blood and of fear.

There was also the creaking and groaning of timber, the wash of the sea, the drag of the sails and the groaning, blaspheming and vomiting of the wounded.

Vella distributed tots of rum, and when Cordelia bandaged the half-naked bleeding seamen, those who were conscious looked at her open-mouthed.

No man expected a woman, and a lady at that, to be occupied with the filthy work of nursing.

To look after wounded men was a man's work, allotted to those who were ordered to do it on account of their incapacity for other jobs, or as a punishment for a bad record.

One of the wounded who was little more than a boy said:

"Be Oi a-dying, Mum?"

After she had reassured him he whispered:

"Only me mother cares for Oi."

Another ship's boy not yet fifteen who was wounded in the arm kept saying:

"Oi were not afraid! Oi were not afraid!"

"Of course you were not!" Cordelia said gently.

It had now been dark for a long time and she had been forced to work by the light of two flickering lanterns before finally she found there were no more patients needing her immediate attention.

There were still a number of the dead lying about on the deck, and now one of the men who had only been stunned by a falling mast helped Vella to commit them to the deep.

As they did so Cordelia heard them murmur:

"*Réquiem aetérnam dona eis, Dómine* – Eternal rest give unto them O Lord," over each body.

Every time as they spoke the beautiful words of the Requiem Mass the two Maltese crossed themselves.

The sea was still getting up and growing rougher, and Cordelia sent Vella below to bring up hammocks and blankets for the men who could not be moved, while a small number were carried down to the lower deck.

It was as they came back from taking down a man who

was only slightly injured in the arm that Vella came to Cordelia and said in a low voice:

"The ship is filling with water, Mistress!"

"Can nothing be done about it?" Cordelia asked.

He shook his head.

"There is no-one to work the pumps and there is already several feet of water in the hold."

Cordelia glanced towards Mark.

They had made him as comfortable as they could with pillows at his back and blankets over him.

Cordelia knew that he should not be moved for fear that his leg would start to bleed again.

She was aware that he had already lost a dangerous amount of blood and there was a great crimson pool beside him on the deck.

"Do not tell the Captain," she murmured.

Vella shook his head.

She told him to take no more men down below, feeling that seamen would rather die in the open than like rats in a trap.

She felt very tired, not only from her labour in tending the wounded, but also from the pitch and roll of the ship and the force of the wind which made it difficult to move about.

It blew her hair around her face and strands of it were being whipped against her cheeks.

Desperately in need of the comfort of his presence, Cordelia sat down beside Mark.

His eyes were closed and she wondered in a sudden panic if he had died.

She put out her hand to touch his forehead and as she did so he said:

"We are – taking in – water!"

She wondered how he knew and felt it must be instinctive.

"A little," she answered. "We are not sinking yet!"

"You – are not – afraid?"

"Not when I am with you."

She moved a little closer to him and slipped her fingers into his.

Then she put her head down on his shoulder and thought that if they had to die she would rather die beside Mark than alone, or in a Maltese prison.

The ship was pitching and listing heavily to port because of dragging its sails. Cordelia reasoned this was why she was not taking in water as quickly as she otherwise might have done.

The holes would be in her starboard side above the water-line but not out of reach of the heavy seas.

There was no moon to-night with a cloudy sky. Occasionally they could see the stars.

The rocking of the ship was almost hypnotic and Cordelia must have slept from sheer exhaustion.

When she opened her eyes the night had gone and although the last stars glimmered faintly above them the dawn was breaking.

She sat up quickly and looked at Mark.

He was awake and his eyes met hers.

It was then, as they looked at each other, there was a sudden terrifying crash and the whole ship heaved and shivered, then heaved again.

Cordelia gave a cry of fear and fell back against Mark.

"We have struck a rock!" he said almost as if speaking to himself.

Now there were a number of voices shouting and crying out. Cordelia pulled herself to her feet and saw that Mark was right.

The ship had been dashed by the seas against the rocks at the foot of a high barren cliff looming above them.

It looked bleak and desolate, and there was only the shrill cry of the gulls and the sound of breaking timber as the ship moved and heaved as if in pain as the seas hit her.

Cordelia looked at the cliffs and realised that it would be impossible even for an able-bodied man to climb them, let alone the wounded lying wet and semi-conscious on the deck.

Vella came running up onto the poop.

"Where do you think we are, Vella?" she asked.

He shrugged his shoulders expressively.

"Perhaps Sicily, Mistress – I do not know – but the ship will not last long. I must try to get you onto the rocks so that you will be safe!"

"Thank you, Vella, but I will not leave the Captain."

"But, Mistress, you are young and unharmed. It would be a waste to die when I can take you to safety."

Vella was knotting a rope as he spoke.

Cordelia shook her head.

"No, Vella, I will stay here. But you save yourself. It is only right that you should do so."

She saw Vella look indecisive, and so that she should not make him feel that he was honour-bound to stay with her she went back to Mark's side and sat down on the deck.

It was impossible anyway to stand; for the ship was shivering and breaking with every sea that struck it.

"What is – happening?"

Mark's voice was strong and she knew that he had fully regained consciousness.

"I am afraid there is nothing we can do," Cordelia answered.

He made an effort as if he would sit up, but she put her hand on his shoulder to hold him still.

"Do not move," she said. "It would be impossible to get ashore or to climb those cliffs."

"You could try."

She smiled at him.

"I prefer to stay with you."

"You have to be saved! You must be saved!"

"There is no chance of that," Cordelia answered gently.

As if to show the truth of her statement a sea seemed to throw the *St. Jude* so violently against the rocks that part of the bow came away and was swept off by the sea.

"I am not afraid," Cordelia said. "I love you, Mark, and we shall be with David."

She bent forward as she spoke and kissed his cold cheek and even as she did so she remembered David reading to her at Stanton Park.

He was always reading about the history of the Knights, but sometimes she did not listen very attentively.

Yet now she remembered a story when the galleys of the Order were nearly swamped by the high seas.

"The sailors," David read, "recited the gospel of St. John with such fervour that the waters quieted down almost immediately!"

'Prayer saved the galleys,' Cordelia thought as she raised her lips from Mark's cheek. 'Why did I not remember before this that prayer could produce miracles if one prayed fervently enough?'

Rising to her feet she staggered to the front of the sloping poop and holding on to the rail she looked down onto the deck strewn with wounded men.

"We are Christians!" she cried and surprisingly her voice was strong and resonant enough to ring out above the noise of the sea. "Let us pray for help, because at this moment there is no-one who can save us but God!"

She took a deep breath, and trying to remember the prayers of the Order that David had recited so often she began:

"Oh, God, who sent Your servant, St. John the Baptist, to be a voice crying in the wilderness to prepare the way for the coming of Christ. Through the intercession of St. John, under whose Cross we sail, save us now in our extremity and, if we cannot be saved, then let us die with the courage that the Knights of the Order have shown all down the centuries."

There was a pause as Cordelia finished speaking, then from the men below and from the poop around her there was the murmur of:

"Good Lord deliver us! St. John, come to our aid!"

She shut her eyes because they were filled with tears.

The prayer had come straight from her heart and she was sure as she spoke that David had put the words into her mind and on her lips.

She turned to go back to Mark, needing to touch him and to know that he was there and because of it she need not be afraid of death.

Then as she turned she looked, blinked her eyes, then looked again.

Coming round the corner of the rocks, not a quarter of a mile away from where they were stranded, was a three-masted ship.

Its sails were billowing out in the breeze and flying at the mast-head was the white ensign!

For a moment Cordelia felt it must be a figment of her imagination.

Then she knew that God and St. John had heard her prayer.

Chapter Seven

Cordelia looked at herself in the mirror and realised her thin white gown was exceedingly becoming, but she was not satisfied.

"I am very pale," she explained to the maid who had helped her to dress.

"You need the sunshine, M'Lady. That's why the doctor says you may go downstairs to-day and lie on the terrace."

It would be a change, Cordelia thought, from her bedroom which while a very attractive one, had begun to seem like a prison this last week.

But the doctor had been insistent that she should not move into the outside world until she was well enough to do so.

"I have been in Naples a long time," she said almost to herself.

"About six weeks, M'Lady. It is August 8th to-day. Two months since the French took Malta!"

It had seemed like two years, because she had not been able to see Mark.

But Lady Hamilton had brought her news of him. He was better, his leg was healing, and he sent a servant to the Embassy every day to make enquiries as to his cousin's health.

After what had been an exhausting voyage back to Naples in *H.M.S. Thunderer* who had rescued them from the Sicilian rocks, Cornelia had collapsed.

She was ashamed of having been so weak, but the anxiety and terror of the battle at sea and the devastation on board the *St. Jude* had taken its toll of her strength.

What was more, while everything was done for her comfort aboard the *H.M.S. Thunderer* she had fought a pitched battle with the ship's Surgeon whose one idea was to cut off the limbs of the wounded men.

"Gangrene will set in, My Lady," he had said positively.

When Cordelia refused to allow him to do his butcher's work, he had stormed off to the Captain to complain of her interference.

Luckily the Captain, who was young and impressionable, was swept off his feet by Cordelia's beauty and was prepared to agree with her rather than with the Surgeon.

Five men died after they were rescued from the *St. Jude* but the rest under Cordelia's ministrations improved daily.

She insisted, despite every protest from the Captain, on herself cleaning and bandaging the wounds of the whole of the *St. Jude*'s crew from the Baron down to the youngest boy.

She felt they were her personal responsibility, and having saved them so far she had no intention of allowing them to die unnecessarily.

"They regard you as an angel of mercy, My Lady," the Captain told her. "If you are not careful you will be canonised!"

"I have no wish to be a saint," Cordelia smiled.

Thinking of Mark, she knew it was the last thing she wanted to be.

He ran a high fever when they were on board the *Thunderer*.

While the doctor was certain it was due to his not having had his leg amputated, Cordelia attributed it to loss of blood and being soaked by the waves breaking over the ship.

He did in fact recover sufficiently when they reached Naples to make arrangements for his men to be taken not to one of the inadequate hospitals in the City, but to a Monastery where the Monks specialised in healing and nursing the sick.

Fortunately as Mark knew the Abbot, this was easily arranged.

Then while Cordelia was taken to the British Embassy, he went to stay with an Italian physician, a friend of his, to whom he was prepared to entrust his wounded leg.

Cordelia learnt that *H.M.S. Thunderer* was part of Nelson's Fleet and had been sent ahead to find out what the position was in Malta and if possible to discover the whereabouts of the French.

The Captain was extremely grateful for all the information that Cordelia was able to give him.

She learnt on arrival that Admiral Nelson himself was outside Naples, desperately trying to obtain food and water for his Fleet, while the King had been forbidden by the French to supply him.

Cordelia having collapsed and nursing a temperature lay in a darkened room and had no knowledge of the drama taking place in the Palazzo Sessa.

But once she was well enough, the story of the anxiety of those tense and dynamic days was related to her by Lady Hamilton.

And how dramatically Her Ladyship told the tale.

When Napoleon had slipped out of Toulon while Nelson was in Sardinia, he had sailed down the Mediterranean like a fox confusing the scent by every means in his power.

Admiral Nelson pursued him hampered by misinformation and by lack of frigates – the scouts of the Fleet – but steadfastly pursuing.

"On that pursuit the fate of Europe hung!" Lady Hamilton cried. "I knew that the British Fleet would need food and water, but what could we do?"

Cordelia learnt that the King had shut himself away in an agony of fear, terrified of a rising in the City, terrified of the French, imagining the guillotine being set up in the Piazza de Mercato and his barbaric splendour being set ablaze about his ears.

"My only hope was the Queen," Lady Hamilton told Cordelia. "We clung together and wept while Sir William argued, pleaded and begged the King for help."

"If he could not obtain water in Naples," Cordelia asked, "where would Admiral Nelson have had to go?"

"Gibraltar was his nearest Port, but by turning back on his tracks he would leave Egypt open to Napoleon."

"What happened?" Cordelia asked breathlessly.

"Admiral Nelson in the *Vanguard* was anchored off Capri.

He sent two of his trusted Captains to Sir William, but there was nothing my husband could do but tell the truth.

"'Gentlemen,' Sir William said, 'I have tried every avenue already to break that most infamous pact forbidding our ships to enter Naples or the Sicilian Ports. I will make further application to the King, but I must be honest and say I am not very optimistic it will succeed.'"

Lady Hamilton drew in her breath.

"It was then I decided to see what I could do and I sought an audience with the Queen."

"She helped you?" Cordelia asked.

She was impatient to hear the end of the story. But Lady Hamilton wished to tell it her own way.

"Sir William came back with a Ministerial Order written under the King's eye, hedged with conditions, barbed with restrictions. The Governors of the Sicilian Ports were to permit the wounded to be taken ashore, but victualling and water were to be accorded only in certain narrowly defined circumstances."

She gave a deep sigh.

"I could see how downcast the Captains were, and I said to Sir William: 'Let us go in our own yacht to call on Admiral Nelson before he puts to sea.'"

"And Sir William agreed?" Cordelia enquired.

"He agreed and it was dusk when we boarded the *Vanguard*. Admiral Nelson greeted us and led the way to his cabin."

"'Has Your Excellency obtained an Order?' he asked Sir William.

"'After a fashion, yes,' Sir William replied, 'but I doubt if it will serve your purpose.'"

"That must have been a blow to the Admiral," Cordelia murmured.

"I saw his face go pale and a tragic expression came into his eyes," Lady Hamilton said. "Then I produced a paper from under my cloak."

"What was it?" Cordelia asked.

"As I explained to Admiral Nelson, the Queen had a seat on the Council. I had urged Her Majesty to use her power.

She feared to do so, but I went down on my knees and beseeched her for the sake of her Kingdom — her children—"

Lady Hamilton's voice broke, as it must have broken when she had ceased to speak in Nelson's cabin and for a moment his white face had swum before her eyes.

"Sir William took the paper from my shaking hand," she said. "He read it, then extended it to the Admiral."

"'I offer you, Sir,' he said, 'from my Lady Hamilton a Royal Order for watering and provisioning the Fleet *where you will*!'"

"I thought for a moment," Lady Hamilton related, "that Admiral Nelson would break down. Then he laid the paper on the table and said in a voice of great solemnity:

"'Madame, you have saved your country. God grant the Fleet may be worthy of your courage and wisdom!'"

It had been a glorious story to listen to, Cordelia thought, but still they did not know the end of it.

As soon as she was better in health she realised that the tension in the Palazzo Sessa increased every hour which passed without news.

There was no disguising the anxiety in Lady Hamilton's beautiful face and Cordelia learnt from the maids who waited on her that worry had made Sir William ill as day after day he waited for a report which never came.

There was always the apprehension that Napoleon's new ships had defeated the older British ones.

Would Admiral Nelson, in bad health, handicapped by the continuous pain he had suffered after the loss of his arm, and with one blind eye, be able to hold his own against the young confident conqueror of Europe?

But at this particular moment Cordelia was concerned only with herself and her appearance.

To-day she would see Mark for the first time since reaching Naples, and she was afraid that he might not be waiting for her with the same impatience which consumed her.

She loved him, she loved him desperately.

Her love was so overwhelming, so complete that it was hard to contemplate he might not feel the same.

What had she to reassure her?

One kiss and the moment on board the *St. Jude* when he had held her in his arms!

She had been prepared to die at his side on the deck of the *St. Jude* but he had been barely conscious at the time and there had been no chance for an intimate conversation aboard the *Thunderer*.

Because of the intense pain he was suffering Mark had been kept asleep most of the two days at sea under the influence of laudanum.

He had roused himself when they reached Naples, but Cordelia had known that it was a superhuman effort on his part and it had left him pale and exhausted when finally he was carried away on a stretcher.

After that she herself remembered little more.

For some days however, she had felt like herself again and to-day the doctor had given her permission to dress and go downstairs.

"You are to lie in the sun, My Lady, and do nothing to exert yourself," he had said severely.

"You are turning me into an invalid!" Cordelia protested, but she had known that what he ordained was sensible.

"The footmen are outside the door, M'Lady," the maid said now, "waiting to carry you down the stairs."

"I can walk!" Cordelia replied indignantly.

"Her Ladyship has arranged for you to be lifted down in a chair."

It was impossible for Cordelia to disregard her hostess's orders.

When she was carried through the Salon onto the terrace outside, she found that with her usual consideration Lady Hamilton had arranged a *chaise-longue* heaped with silk cushions under a canvas awning which would protect her from the heat of the sun.

The view of the Bay and the flowers rioting in the garden were even lovelier, Cordelia thought, than she remembered.

It was almost unreal in its beauty, like a scene from a play! Was she the heroine?

She felt a little tremor of fear in case, in her longing and need of Mark, she had built up a false image of his response.

But she had hardly been alone for more than five minutes before the Major Domo's voice announced in stentorian tones :

"The Earl of Hunstanton to see you, M'Lady!"

Cordelia gave a start.

She had forgotten that Mark had inherited the title from David and that his position in life was now very different from what it had been before.

Then any thought about his title was swept away with an inexpressible gladness as he appeared.

He looked thinner and his face had lost a little of its tan, but his eyes were brilliantly blue.

The only difference was that instead of walking lithely and quickly in the athletic manner to which she was accustomed, he came towards her slowly, leaning on an ivory-handled walking stick.

There was so much she had planned to say to him, so much she had rehearsed in her mind; but now the words were swept from her lips.

She could only stare at him, her eyes very large in her small face.

"You are well?" he asked.

She had forgotten how deep his voice was and that it vibrated through her so that she felt as if it was a note of music to which she must respond.

"Is your leg . . . better?"

"Thanks entirely to you I still have it!"

"Does it hurt?"

"Only when I stand."

"Then sit down," Cordelia said quickly. "You must rest . . . you must take care of yourself."

He smiled and it made him look younger.

"There is so much I want to say to you, Cordelia," he began, "but first I must thank you."

"No . . . please . . ." she protested.

"How could I imagine that any woman could be so courageous, so amazingly and unbelievably wonderful?"

Cordelia felt the colour flood into her cheeks.

Because she was shy her eyes fell before his and she could

look only at his leg, heavily dressed, and remember the terrifying open wound which she had bandaged on board the *St. Jude*.

Mark was here, near her as she had wanted, but he was so large, so overwhelming, that he made her tremble.

"Is the Baron very depressed about the loss of his ship?" she asked inconsequently.

"He is so deeply grateful to be alive that everything else is of little importance," Mark replied.

"I hear he is . . . better."

"I went to see him yesterday and in a short while he will be well enough to return home to his family."

"That is good news," Cordelia said, "and the seamen?"

"Several have already recovered enough to go to sea again, and they were all very grateful for the fruit and delicacies you sent them."

Cordelia hesitated, then she said tentatively :

"As they lost . . . the prize money . . . I wondered . . ."

Mark smiled.

"I have already seen to that. It was a thanks offering, and as you know I am now a rich man. But I am hoping you do not resent my taking David's place."

"No, no, of course not!" Cordelia replied. "I am so glad it is . . . you. And I hated to think of Stanton Park shut up and the estate . . . neglected."

Mark bent forward towards her.

"Cordelia—" he began.

Her heart missed a beat. She felt that he was about to say something of such significance that she held her breath.

At that moment they were interrupted.

Lady Hamilton came out of the Salon onto the terrace.

"My dears," she exclaimed. "How delightful it is to have you both here! Please do not rise, My Lord. I do not intend to stay more than a few moments. Sir William needs me."

She put her white hand on Mark's shoulder and said with a smile :

"I am sure you two have a great deal to talk about. I will see that you are not disturbed. Be careful of the sun. It is very hot to-day!"

She walked to the balustrade of the terrace as if to confirm that she was not exaggerating. Then she gave a little cry.

"A ship! An English ship making harbour!"

Even as she spoke there was a salute to the Royal flag at St. Elmo and the forts replied.

"It must be news!" Lady Hamilton said. "News of Admiral Nelson and the British Fleet. Pray God that we will not be disappointed!"

Mark rose from his chair to stand beside her.

A boat was putting out from the ship which had dropped anchor near the shore.

"Do you think there has been a battle?" Lady Hamilton asked in an agonised whisper. "Perhaps the French ships have eluded them again. Oh, God, how can I stand the suspense?"

"It will not be long now," Mark said consolingly.

They watched the boat reach the Quay. Then they heard a cheer in the distance – the screeching foreign cheer which had often amused Lady Hamilton.

She had laughed about it with Admiral Nelson.

The sound came nearer, gathered volume and grew louder and louder.

Naples was yelling for joy – but why? And what for?

Without a word Lady Hamilton turned and ran from the terrace.

Mark walked back to Cordelia who had not moved.

"I will find out what is happening," he said.

She saw that he too was anxious, and as he turned to leave her his lips were set in the line she knew so well which meant he was exerting a strong control over his feelings.

Passing through the Salon Mark found that Lady Hamilton had gone to the entrance of the Embassy.

She was standing on the steps and joining her from every part of the Palazzo Sessa were the servants, clerks and secretaries.

All were aware that something momentous was occurring although everyone was afraid to put a name to it.

Mark could not move quickly and when at length he

reached Lady Hamilton's side he saw two naval Officers walking swiftly and steadily towards them looking neither to the right nor to the left.

Outside the wrought-iron gates the crowds had stopped, but they were still yelling and cheering.

Mark recognised Captain Hoste and Captain Capel, two of Nelson's most valued commanders. He knew them both.

They saw Lady Hamilton and came to the bottom of the steps almost at a run.

"What is it?"

It was doubtful whether they could have heard her question, because the words seemed to be strangled in her throat.

"Madam, a great and glorious victory. The French Fleet is destroyed!"

Even as the words left Captain Hoste's lips, the strain she had felt these last weeks seemed to snap in Emma Hamilton's mind.

She flung up her arms and fainted dead away, falling heavily on the marble steps.

The Captains and the servants carried her to the room nearest the entrance, but as they laid her down her eye-lids fluttered and the colour came back into her cheeks.

The story of the battle was to be told over and over again, but at that moment all that mattered was that Admiral Nelson had found the French Fleet anchored in Aboukir Bay.

He had given the signal to attack on the afternoon of August 1st.

Admiral de Brueys in command of the French Fleet had been unable to get his ships into the abandoned and neglected port.

"He offered ten thousand *lires* to any pilot who would guide his flotilla into harbour," Captain Capel related.

"But he had to anchor in the open road-stead, lying in a long line moored stern to stern, in what was considered an impregnable position," Captain Hoste interposed.

Everyone was listening breathlessly as the Captains went on to tell how the French ships had 1,096 cannons and 11,230 men.

"A north-west wind bore our Fleet towards the French at half past six in the evening," Captain Hoste said. "By a brilliant and unexpected manoeuvre the *Goliath* and the *Zealous*, followed by several more, got between the French ships and the shore.

"That meant," Captain Capel explained, seeing that Lady Hamilton did not understand, "that they could escape the French gunfire for all their cannons were pointing seaward!"

Lady Hamilton clasped her hands together.

"The French ships," Captain Capel continued, "were immobile and now caught as if 'between a pair of nut-crackers'. Sir Horatio opened a murderous cannonade and the French were raked by our broad-sides from both flanks. We fought all night!"

"And the British losses?" Mark asked.

They were the first words he had spoken since the Captains had begun their tale.

"Heavy!" Captain Hoste replied. "The great ships were so closely engaged that every cannonade swept off victims. Three times the gunners on the *Vanguard* were dragged away dead."

"But so skilfully had the British plan been made," Captain Hoste continued, "that our battle-line remained unbroken as our ships steadily moved forward along each side of the line. One by one the French ships, though they fought obstinately, succumbed."

There was a moment's silence, then Captain Capel said tentatively:

"Sir Horatio had only just received the news of the last surrender when he was hit by a stray shot."

Lady Hamilton gave a cry of horror.

"He was wounded, but not dangerously," Captain Hoste explained quickly, "while the French Admiral was killed!"

"The French fought bravely," Captain Capel conceded. "One of their frigates blew herself up, five were sunk and over four thousand Frenchmen died that night! There was however one regrettable loss."

"What was that?" Mark asked.

"*L'Orient* was set on fire and when the fire reached the powder magazines the whole ship went sky high!"

"That was a pity," Mark said laconically. "The prize-money would have been tremendous!"

Lady Hamilton rose from the couch on which she had been lying.

"I must write to Admiral Nelson, but first, Gentlemen, I will take you to the Palace at Caserta. The Queen must hear what you have to relate."

She ran to the door and called to the servants:

"My cloak! My hat! Order a carriage!"

And a few minutes later, having told Sir William the stupendous news, she left the Palazzo Sessa with the two Captains.

Mark went back to Cordelia.

As he appeared she watched him wide-eyed until he was close to her. Then she held out her hand.

"I know by your expression that it is a victory!"

"A great victory!" he agreed. "But before I tell you all about it, before anything else interrupts us, I have a question to ask you."

"What is it?" she enquired.

His fingers tightened on hers, and he said gravely:

"Will you, my darling, marry me immediately?"

*   *   *

Cordelia looked around the Sitting-Room and gave a little sigh of delight.

Despite the heat outside, the white walls and the sun-blinds over the open windows left the room cool.

There were flowers everywhere, with great bowls of fragrant blossom on low tables and on Grecian pillars which Cordelia knew would have delighted Sir William.

It was due to him that they had been provided with this small but exquisite Villa for their honeymoon.

Lady Hamilton had suggested that they should go to the Ambassador's summer residence at Caserta.

But Sir William with a diplomatic perception had realised

they would find the proximity of the Royal Family and the house which he had enlarged overpowering, when all Cordelia and Mark wanted was to be alone.

He had therefore persuaded one of his archaeologist friends to lend them his Villa built on the coast only a few miles from Naples. It had not taken long for the bridal couple to drive there from the Palazzo Sessa.

The ceremony had been very quiet, attended only by Sir William and Lady Hamilton.

It was Cordelia's wish that there should be no curious strangers to watch her pledge herself to Mark, and she was moreover in mourning.

It would have been correct to wait for some months after David's death before she married.

But Mark had asked her to marry him immediately so that they could return to England together on the ship which was carrying the reports of Nelson's victory to the Admiralty.

She had known that he would allow none of the conventional reasons to delay her from being his wife.

The ship was to leave in three days' time.

They would, therefore, have a very short honeymoon, but Cordelia was sure it would be a perfect one.

She was aware that Mark had been afraid she would think he was hurrying her, but she loved him so overwhelmingly that she was convinced however long they waited she could not love him more.

She had known from the expression in his eyes that he had been afraid of her answer. But her reply was very simple.

"As soon as you . . . want me."

She had felt his lips on her hand.

Then his mouth sought hers and all the rapture and ecstasy she had known the first time he had kissed her seemed to mingle with the sunshine and the flowers.

The wonder of it was part of the lucidity of light which hung over the Bay.

Mark raised his head.

"I love you, my darling! I love you!"

She had known then that she already belonged to him and they were no longer two people but one.

*　　　*　　　*

Their wedding in an ancient Church which had an atmosphere redolent with the faith of countless worshippers had been to Cordelia so sacred and so beautiful that she felt those she had loved were there beside them.

She was certain of her mother's presence and of David's.

She had thought too that perhaps the spirits of the men who had died on the *St. Jude* were not far from them.

They had admired and respected Mark and they would have wanted his happiness.

"I will make him happy," Cordelia vowed. "Help me . . . God, please . . . help me."

She knew that never again would she doubt the validity of prayer when a miracle had saved them from drifting on the rocks of Sicily.

When the Priest who married them pronounced the blessing she thanked God in her heart for having blessed them already in that they were both alive.

As they drove back to the Palazzo Sessa in an open carriage Mark had held her hand tightly in his.

There had been no need for words. They were both filled with a mystic happiness, so holy, so perfect, that spiritually they were one.

At the British Embassy they had an early meal, cut a wedding cake made by the Chef, and responded to the toast Sir William drank to them in champagne.

Then, pelted with rose petals by the staff, they had said good-bye and been carried in the Ambassador's carriage to the Villa on the Bay.

Cordelia turned towards Mark with a smile.

"It is so beautiful!" she exclaimed. "Look at the vases, which must make Sir William quite envious, the Greek pillars, and that adorable little stone statue. Do you not find it exquisite?"

"There is only one thing I wish to look at, at the moment and it is breathtakingly exquisite."

He put his arms around her.

Because she thrilled at his touch and at the same time feeling shy at the intensity of her own feelings, she said impetuously:

"Let us go and look at the garden. I am told it is very lovely."

"We will see it later on, when it is cooler," Mark answered. "This is the hottest time of the day and you have to rest."

"I have no wish to do that," Cordelia said quickly.

"The doctor instructed me that you are not to do too much too quickly," Mark insisted, "and you have already done a lot this morning."

"I have been married for . . . one thing!"

"You must tell me about it later!" Mark smiled. "But now I want you to rest."

"And if I do not want to?"

"You have promised to obey me!"

She looked at him mischievously, wanting to tease him because he was so solemn.

"Suppose I forget my vows and disobey your august commands?"

"Then I will have to punish you — with kisses!"

He pulled her closely against him.

His lips were on hers and it was impossible to move, impossible to do anything but feel the rapture he aroused.

She felt her body melt into his as she drew closer and still closer to him.

But while she longed for him to go on kissing her he released her to say in a voice which was slightly unsteady:

"Go and rest, Cordelia. I insist upon it!"

"When I am lying down will you come and talk to me?"

"Only for a moment," he replied. "Then I too will rest."

"In that case I will be . . . good."

Cordelia thought perhaps his leg was hurting him and remembered he had done a lot of walking and standing during the morning.

"I must take care of him," she told herself.

One of the advantages of the Villa, as Sir William had

pointed out, was that the bed-rooms were on the ground floor and Mark would therefore not have to struggle up and down stairs.

Cordelia's bed-room was white like the Sitting-Room. The big bed was draped with muslin curtains falling from a corola of dancing cupids.

All the flowers were white too.

Lilies and roses scented the air and here too the open windows looked out over the colourful garden to the shimmering sea.

There was a young Neapolitan maid who was, Cordelia knew, the daughter of the couple who staffed the Villa, to help her take off her white wedding-gown.

She had worn nothing elaborate. But of muslin and lace, it was a very beautiful dress and she intended to treasure it all her life.

'I will wear it every year on the occasion of our anniversary,' she planned.

She had known when she had joined Mark in the Church there had been admiration as well as love in his eyes.

She looked down at the ring encircling her third finger and thought its unbroken circle was symbolic of their marriage which would last for ever.

"We will grow closer and even happier as the years go by," Cordelia whispered.

She could think of nothing more wonderful than to live with Mark at Stanton Park which, the background of her life hitherto, she had always loved.

He had always seemed to belong there and now it was his.

She had the unshakable feeling that David would be as glad as she was that Mark should carry on the long line of Stantons who had lived in Berkshire and played their part in the service of their country.

There had been no time to discuss such matters.

But now that Mark would no longer be able to go to sea Cordelia knew that he would find an outlet for his energy in Politics and in the important County appointments which would be waiting for him when they reached home.

The fact that he was now head of the family carried both responsibilities and problems.

"He will do it all so perfectly!" she told herself.

Having been deep in her thoughts, she had not realised that the maid had taken away her clothes.

Now she was wearing a thin, diaphanous nightgown of muslin and lace, covered with a négligée to match which was ornamented with tiny bows of blue ribbon, symbolic of good fortune.

It was too hot to get into bed and Cordelia lay on top of it, her back against the soft pillows, with only the cover of fine lace to hide her naked feet.

The maid curtseyed and withdrew.

The room was very quiet save for the gentle murmur of the bees buzzing among the flowers in the garden.

The door opened and Mark came in.

He was wearing the long white cotton robe with a coloured sash in which the Neapolitans took their siestas.

He must have borrowed it, Cordelia thought, from the owner of the Villa because the initials embroidered on the pocket were not his own.

But it became him and as he walked slowly, limping a little, towards her she thought how handsome he was. There was something about him that always reminded her irresistibly of a Knight.

"Come and sit down," she said. "You know you should not be walking without a stick."

Mark looked for a chair and not finding one sat down on the bed, facing Cordelia.

She put out her hands towards him.

"Are you . . . happy?" she asked.

"It is impossible for me to find words to tell you how happy," he replied. "There are so many things I want to tell you, my precious darling, but it is difficult for me to know how to begin."

"What sort of things?" she asked.

"First that you are the most beautiful person I have ever seen! Secondly that you are the bravest, the kindest and quite the most perfect woman I could ever imagine!"

"You are . . . making me . . . shy," Cordelia protested.

"I love you when you are shy," Mark answered. "I did not realise when we talked together in the garden at the Embassy that you were everything I had looked for all my life, but which I had always failed to find."

"I think actually you found me rather . . . tiresome."

"No, never tiresome, but I did not expect to find so much wisdom in that little golden head, nor did I ever imagine I would fall in love with a young girl."

"Perhaps . . . because I am . . . ignorant about so many things . . . I will bore you?" Cordelia said in a low voice.

Mark smiled.

"That is impossible. You know as well as I do, my lovely wife, that we are an indivisible part of each other!"

"You are . . . sure of . . . that?" Cordelia asked, her eyes on his.

"As sure as I am that it was your prayers and your faith in God which brought us to safety," he said quietly.

Cordelia's fingers tightened on his.

"It was after you . . . kissed me in Malta that I realised I . . . loved you! But afterwards I knew I had loved you . . . a long time before . . . that."

There was a dazzling light in her eyes as she went on:

"When you were so kind and understanding . . . when you explained to me that real love was divine, the dream we hold in our hearts, I fell in love."

"And my dream has come true."

There was a deep note in Mark's voice as he raised her hands to his lips.

He kissed the backs of them, then turning them over he kissed the palms, his mouth passionate and possessive.

She felt a thrill streak through her which was half rapture and half an exquisite pain.

Her lips were aching for his and there was a flame flickering inside her which grew more insistent every time he touched her, every time she heard that deep note in his voice.

"I must let you sleep, my precious one," Mark said, "but before I leave you there is one thing I want to say."

Again his tone was very solemn and Cordelia looked at him wide-eyed but with a touch of apprehension.

"It is this," he went on. "We have been married in a great hurry, before you are really well, before we have had time to talk about ourselves and really get to know each other."

He paused before he continued:

"It was expedient because now I can take you back to England safely in a battle-ship."

His hand tightened on hers as he said fiercely:

"Never again will I risk your life, my sweet darling, never again as long as you live shall you encounter the perils you experienced on the *St. Jude*."

"I want you to be . . . safe too," Cordelia replied. "But what are you . . . trying to . . . say to me?"

"I am trying to say in a rather long-winded manner," Mark said with a brief smile, "that because I love you so overwhelmingly, I will do nothing which might frighten or perhaps shock you."

"I could never be frightened or shocked by you," Cordelia answered. "But I still do not . . . understand . . ."

"We are married, my adorable wife, but if you think we should wait a little before I make love to you, I will do so, although it will be hard."

"Are you . . . saying," Cordelia asked in a very small voice, "that you do not . . . want me?"

His fingers gripped hers so hard that she almost cried out with the pain.

"Not want you! I want you as I have never wanted a woman in the whole of my life!"

He drew in his breath.

"I want you not only because I adore your beauty and your exquisite perfect body! My love is far greater than that! I love you in a way I have never loved before. I worship you, Cordelia. I know now what stands in the shrine within my heart. It is you!"

Cordelia felt the wonder of what he was saying sweep over her so that the whole room seemed to be filled with light and she and Mark were enveloped by it.

Then she took her hands from his and put them around his neck.

"I love . . . you, too!" she whispered. "I love you in the . . . same way that you . . . love me. You fill . . . the whole world."

She drew him a little nearer as she said:

"I do not need to . . . wait to know you . . . better. I know you now and you are all I have . . . longed for . . . all I have . . . dreamt of. To be with you . . . is to be in . . . Heaven."

"My beloved, you should not say such things to me," Mark said and his voice was hoarse.

Then, as if he could not help himself or resist the invitation of Cordelia's arms, his mouth came down on hers.

He was trying to be gentle, he was trying, she knew, to keep control of himself.

But a flame within her seemed to leap higher and as it rose it ignited a fire in him, so that his kisses became fierce, demanding, masterful and wildly passionate.

He kissed her eyes, her cheeks, her ears and the softness of her neck so that she quivered with sensations she had never dreamt existed.

"My wonderful, brave, perfect little wife!" he murmured and pulled aside the lace négligée to kiss her breasts.

Everything seemed to vanish except the insistence and wonder of his lips. She could feel his heart beating.

"You are mine! Mine for eternity and beyond!"

Her body moved beneath his.

Then there was only the ecstasy of their dreams and the Divine glory which came from God.

Other Books by Barbara Cartland

Romantic Novels, over 150, the most recently published being :

An Arrow to the Heart
The Elusive Earl
The Blue Eyed Witch
A Dream from the Night
Never Laugh at Love
The Secret of the Glen

Autobiographical and Biographical

The Isthmus Years 1919–1939
The Years of Opportunity 1939–1945
I Search for Rainbows 1945–1966
We Danced All Night 1919–1929
Ronald Cartland (with a foreword by Sir Winston Churchill)
Polly, My Wonderful Mother

Historical

Bewitching Women
The Outrageous Queen
(The Story of Queen Christina of Sweden)
The Scandalous Life of King Carol
The Private Life of King Charles II
The Private Life of Elizabeth, Empress of Austria
Josephine, Empress of France
Diane de Poitiers
Metternich – the Passionate Diplomat

Sociology

You in the Home
The Fascinating Forties
Marriage for Moderns
Be Vivid, Be Vital
Love, Life and Sex
Vitamins for Vitality
Husbands and Wives
Etiquette

The Many Facets of Love
Sex and the Teenager
The Book of Charm
Living Together
The Youth Secret
Barbara Cartland's Book of Beauty and Health
Men are Wonderful

Cookery

Barbara Cartland's Health Food Cookbook
Food for Love
The Magic of Honey

Editor of

The Common Problems by Ronald Cartland
(with a preface by the Rt. Hon. The Earl of Selborne, P.C.)

Drama

Blood Money
French Dressing

Philosophy

Touch the Stars

Radio Operetta

The Rose and the Violet (music by Mark Lubbock)
Performed in 1942

Radio Plays

The Caged Bird : An episode in the Life of Elizabeth,
Empress of Austria. Performed in 1957

Verse

Lines on Life and Love

Other Pan books that may interest you
are listed on the following pages

Georgette Heyer

Beauvallet 70p

Sir Nicholas Beauvallet, friend of Drake and a favourite of the Queen, had never engaged on a more reckless venture – his sword and wits against all Spain . . . And Nick's first meeting with the lovely Dona Dominica de Rada y Sylva on the bloodstained deck of a captured galleon was nearly as dangerous for his peace of mind.

Black Sheep 70p

Abigail Wendover was determined to prevent Fanny, her pretty, high-spirited niece, from being gulled into a clandestine marriage with Stacy Calverleigh, an acknowledged fortune-hunter. The arrival of Stacy's uncle seemed to bring an ally – but Miles turned out to be a most provoking creature.

The Foundling 75p

Despite his fortune Gilly, the young Duke of Sale, was bored – he longed to give his adoring household the slip, to sample the robustness of Regency life as plain Mr Dash. When he gets away Gilly finds himself plunged into a world of footpads, duels, chases – and the beautiful Belinda, a blackmailer's decoy . . .

Venetia 75p

Lord Damerel found Venetia the most engaging and wittily perverse female he had encountered in his thirty-eight years. Venetia knew her neighbour for a gamester, a rake, a man of sadly unsteady character. So it was provoking to find that, at times, he could be quite idiotically noble . . .

Juliette Benzoni
Marianne and the Masked Prince 70p

After many exciting adventures, Marianne conquers Paris – mistress of Napoleon, beloved by the Imperial Guard, star of the Opéra Comique . . .

Suddenly, her dearly won happiness is threatened by Francis Cranmere, the husband whom she thought dead.

And the Emperor has eyes only for Marie-Louise, his new Empress.

In desperation Marianne journeys to Tuscany, home of a mysterious masked prince whose magnificent palace harbours the unholy rituals of Black Magic . . .

Marianne and the Privateer 60p

Fleeing from her second husband, the mysterious masked Prince Sant'Anna, and the hidden evils of his Tuscany estates, Marianne returns to the pomp and vice of the Emperor's Paris.

Once again, men fight over her breathtaking beauty, but Marianne's heart is lost to Jason Beaufort, the bold American sea-rover.

Enmeshed in a web of dangerous intrigue, Marianne finds her new love threatened by the lust of Count Chernychev, the greed of Francis Cranmere, the ambitions of Napoleon and the vengeance of Pilar – spurned wife to Jason . . .

Selected bestsellers

☐ **The Eagle Has Landed** Jack Higgins 80p
☐ **The Moneychangers** Arthur Hailey 95p
☐ **Marathon Man** William Goldman 70p
☐ **Nightwork** Irwin Shaw 75p
☐ **Tropic of Ruislip** Leslie Thomas 75p
☐ **One Flew Over The Cuckoo's Nest** Ken Kesey 75p
☐ **Collision** Spencer Dunmore 70p
☐ **Perdita's Prince** Jean Plaidy 70p
☐ **The Eye of the Tiger** Wilbur Smith 80p
☐ **The Shootist** Glendon Swarthout 60p
☐ **Of Human Bondage** Somerset Maugham 95p
☐ **Rebecca** Daphne du Maurier 80p
☐ **Slay Ride** Dick Francis 60p
☐ **Jaws** Peter Benchley 70p
☐ **Let Sleeping Vets Lie** James Herriot 60p
☐ **If Only They Could Talk** James Herriot 60p
☐ **It Shouldn't Happen to a Vet** James Herriot 60p
☐ **Vet In Harness** James Herriot 60p
☐ **Tinker Tailor Soldier Spy** John le Carré 75p
☐ **Gone with the Wind** Margaret Mitchell £1.75
☐ **Cashelmara** Susan Howatch £1.25
☐ **The Nonesuch** Georgette Heyer 60p
☐ **The Grapes of Wrath** John Steinbeck 95p
☐ **Drum** Kyle Onstott 60p

All these books are available at your bookshop or newsagent;
or can be obtained direct from the publisher
Just tick the titles you want and fill in the form below
Prices quoted are applicable in UK
Pan Books, Cavaye Place, London SW10 9PG
Send purchase price plus 15p for the first book and 5p for
each additional book, to allow for postage and packing

Name _____
(block letters please)

Address _____

_____

While every effort is made to keep prices low, it is sometimes
necessary to increase prices at short notice. Pan Books reserve the
right to show on covers new retail prices which may differ
from those advertised in the text or elsewhere